Midwinter at Bhisho

by

Earl T. Roske

Seasons of War on Abira
Book 1

Cover by: Mike Beckstrom

Thank You:
Tim, Andrew, Nicole, Mike, Erin,
Trish, Megan

And the Beta Readers!
Wendy
Kathy
AsiaMan

For my wife and daughter.
&
Judy, my mom.
20 November 1943 – 14 March 2019
Never forgotten,
Always Remembered.

01

Sergeant Imara Fermo slowly turned in a circle. Even though her eyes were closed, she could see the bright winter light through her eyelids. On her cheeks, she felt the biting cold of the winter wind as it blew through the Saastal valley. She kept turning, waiting.

"Okay," a voice said. Cpl Bowers, the one who seemed to enjoy this the most.

Imara stopped turning. Something cold touched her nose, leaving a wet feeling behind. In the near distance, she could hear the voices of other Hospitallers and the crunch of snow as more crawlers emerged from the bellies of the dropships and rolled across the ground on their wide tractor treads.

If she were to open her eyes, which would displease Cpl Bowers and the others, she would have to adjust the density filter on her face shield. Without the adjustment, everything would be washed out, the snow-buried hedgerows, outbuildings, and stone fences lost in more than just several feet of snow. Not to mention that if she did open her eyes, they would want her to spin again. They were already wasting time.

"Any day, Cpl Bowers," Imara said. "We still have work to do."

"I know, Sarge." Bowers had moved. Imara knew Bowers had been standing to the east of Imara. Now, her voice came from a different location, south-southeast. As if that would make this any more difficult. "Just orienting my heads-up display. Right, here we go. Point north, Sgt Fermo."

Imara turned to point to where her back had been facing. There was no hesitation in her movement. She knew where north was despite only being on Abira less than two hours. Several people chuckled.

"Now, the town, Sgt Fermo, where is it?"

Imara moved her hand several degrees counterclockwise and stopped. Her hand pointed unwaveringly in the direction of Bhisho. It was the reason the Hospitallers had brought supplies.

"Crazy, right?" Cpl Bower asked.

Her question was the signal that the little game was over. Imara opened her eyes and looked around. Something cold and wet kissed her cheek. The snow had started again. And though she had no doubt, she verified that she'd gotten both directions correct. It was a rare moment when she didn't. So rare that she could recall each and every time.

The last time she remembered being wrong was when the dropship she'd been in had gone into a wild spin. One of the engines was damaged by enemy fire, and they landed off target. All of their electronics had been fried. They'd used Imara's sense of direction to find their way to the front. She'd missed their company's location by fifty meters after traveling two kilometers across the war-battered ground.

"That's amazing," said one of the people in Cpl Bowers's fireteam, Pfc Isaac Sullivan. He was new to the unit, joining them just before the jump to Abira space. He was the reason Bowers just had to play the little game.

"Could be luck," suggested someone else.

Everyone turned to see Lt Guadalupe White approaching.

"Squad! Attention!" Imara snapped her feet together, the click of her heels muffled by the snow, and saluted the lieutenant.

"Stand easy," said Lt White as she returned the salute. "So, is it luck?"

Cpl Bowers laughed. "No way, Lt White. I've seen Sgt Fermo do this too many times. She could find her way in the dark with her eyes closed."

"Why would she have to close her eyes if the room is dark?" Pvt Wade Rodriguez asked. He'd wandered over from where his fireteam leader, Cpl Brandon Larson, was checking tie-downs on the side of one of the four crawlers in Imara's squad.

"Just to make it more difficult," Pfc Sarah Harmon said. She punched Pvt Rodriguez's arm for emphasis.

"I know." He gave Pfc Harmon an easy push in retaliation.

Imara smiled at the interplay even though she knew one day it could be a problem. There was no doubting the attraction between Harmon and Rodriguez. Fraternization among the ranks wasn't disallowed, but within a squad, it was a problem. If anyone knew from experience, Imara knew. Her hand traveled, seemingly of its own accord, to the pocket where she carried two pocket knives. They were the ones given to Hospitaller orphans on their fifteenth birthday. Everyone was given one. The second knife that Imara carried was not hers and weighed like an anchor on her conscience.

Harmon and Rodriguez, though. The affection was there but not yet intimate. As this was primarily an aid and comfort mission, Imara would let it ride for now. She'd deal with the growing relationship when they were back onboard the dropship carrier, Armengol. For now, they had a job to do.

"Bowers! Larson!" Imara said. Her voice was raised to be heard over the activity around the crawlers and the whine of the dropship engines coming back online. "We tied down and ready to move?"

Imara's question was like a signal to the rest of the squad. They hustled over to the crawlers they were responsible for.

"Crawler one, crawler two ready to go," said Cpl Bowers.

"Three, four, ready," said Cpl Larson.

"Okay, Sgt Fermo," said Lt White. "Let's move forward fifty meters and give the ships room to lift."

"On it, Lieutenant."

Lt White nodded and turned, speaking into her comm. Ten meters away, four more crawlers jumped with activity. Twelve crawlers for first platoon. Second platoon, further down the line of waking dropships, began to move their twelve crawlers out of the lift zone.

Imara turned to her squad. They watched her, waiting for a

command. "Let's move. Fifty meters."

"Yes, Sgt Fermo." It was a ragged response, highlighted by a cheeriness that often infected the voices of the Orphan Corps.

Whether by war, natural disaster, or other events, every soldier in the Orphan Corps was an orphan. That had been the original intention of the Hospitallers. They took in the orphans that seemed to be an inevitable by-product of the wars. Wars that seemed to bubble up with the consistency of air pockets at the bottom of a pot of boiling water.

Originally, when the Hospitallers came into being over three hundred standard years ago, the care of orphans was the only mission. But as the children grew up, they needed something to do with their lives. So, the Hospitallers evolved into an aid organization, bringing medical attention and food supplies to towns, cities, continents, planets damaged by disasters, natural and those made by humans.

With time and expanded missions, the Hospitallers found themselves frequently caught up in wars, taking their own losses as a consequence. When they took it upon themselves to defend against attack, the leadership realized the mission needed to be expanded. Thus, the Orphan Corps was created.

What had once been 'aid and comfort' evolved once more and became 'aid, comfort, defend.' They took to the new mission with vigor and enthusiasm, becoming one of the top military forces in the second radial arm of the galaxy. Even the United Planet System Marines would admit, after several bottles of good quality beer, that the Orphan Corps were a force to be reckoned with.

At the moment, though, Imara was certain that her squad would like to reckon with a hot cup of Insta and a warm blanket despite the heating system built into their uniforms.

"How cold is it?" bellowed Pfc Bruce Cummings. He tended to have only one volume from Imara's experience as his squad leader.

"Negative three," answered Cpl Bowers.

Bowers was walking next to Pfc Harmon. Harmon was focused on the heads-up display that only she could see on her helmet's face shield. Her hands were extended outward, manipulating the augmented reality controls that no one else could see. Walking and manipulating AR controls wasn't a natural pairing. Therefore, most of Harmon's focus was primarily on the crawler controls, Bowers was there in case she tripped.

"Negative three? It's freezing out here," Pfc Cummings said. Again, his voice was loud enough and had such a low timber that if they were close to the steep hills around the valley, he'd likely have caused an avalanche.

"Negative three," said Pfc Isaac Sullivan, the last member of Bowers' fireteam. "That's below freezing, Cummings."

"Still freezing," Cummings bellowed back.

Imara shook her head, but the smile stayed on her face. She turned and walked over to crawler three. Cpl Larson was walking next to Pfc Isabel Schultz, who was operating the crawler's AR controls.

"I hear it's freezing," Cpl Larson said as he looked in Imara's direction.

"How could you not hear that," said Pfc Schultz, her eyes still on the HUD and front end of the crawler.

The crawlers were flat transport machines. They carried cargo through every situation, whether it be snow or swamp. Crawlers were almost as wide as they were long. They were also one of the earliest designs developed by the Hospitaller systems. They rarely malfunctioned. Occasionally, Hospitallers rode on them. But this time, they were stacked five meters tall with emergency foods and other aid supplies for the town of Bhisho. So, the Hospitallers walked.

"Yes," said Imara, "it's cold."

Not that any of them was actually discomforted by the below-freezing weather. They might not be dressed in white winter combat, but the grays they did have on were winter designed. They had internal heating systems that kept them comfortable from the tops of their heads to the tips of their toes. If any of those not controlling a crawler wanted, they could have dropped their face shield and pulled up the facemasks built into the collars of their uniforms.

"Ten meters to go," Schultz said. She looked up and then back down, turning the crawler several degrees to starboard.

The dropships had come down in the fields that wrapped themselves around the town of Bhisho. The fields were divided by hedgerows and fences that were mere bumps and ridges under the meter of snow that was on the ground. The Hospitaller command had apologized in advance for the damage that landing dropships in the fields would cause. The town leaders didn't complain, eager to finally have more than starvation rations.

But that didn't mean the Hospitallers could just destroy anything along the way. It wasn't just rude, it wasn't the Hospitaller way. People tended to be more agreeable and trusting when help didn't bust up everything on the way in.

Pfc Shultz's actions with the crawler had been performed to avoid a hump of snow that could have been a hedgerow or small outbuilding. To the left of them, the other fireteam had done the opposite, steering their crawlers to port. They came around the mysterious lump and then converged, stopping at the fifty-meter mark.

"All right, standby," Imara said. She tapped the comm, addressing Lt White. "First squad in position, Lieutenant."

"Good to hear, Fermo. You might want to move your people to the leeward side of the crawlers. Dropships departing imminently."

Imara motioned to her people. "Leeward, unless you like being in a blizzard."

She trudged around the side of the third crawler, followed by Cpl Larson's fireteam. Behind them, she could hear the increasing whine of the dropships as they built up the energy to push against the planet's gravity and to the carrier waiting in geosynchronous orbit. A last look before ducking behind the crawler showed the dropships rapidly disappearing behind small hurricanes of snow pulled up from the ground and swirled about.

"I miss my bunk already." Pfc Cummings' voice was clear even through the distance between the crawlers and the budding roar of the dropships as they left the ground.

If someone answered Cummings, Imara didn't hear. The dropships were now fifty-plus meters overhead and climbing, the noise of their lift engines finally loud enough to cut off

Cummings' loud voice. Snow billowed past and over the crawlers. It was a momentary whiteout where Imara could see nothing but snow. She dropped her face shield and suggested to the rest of her squad they do the same.

Within minutes, the ships were glowing dots, disappearing into the thick, white clouds that seemed as stationary as the carrier waiting in space above. Imara kicked her way through the powdery snow deposited from the dropships' takeoff and made her way around to the other side. Down the line, all of the crawlers were blanketed on the windward side by slowly settling blankets of snow.

It was a lot of snow in Imara's opinion. She'd seen winter action on a few planets. But nothing quite like this. According to the ruling government of Abira, this wasn't a usual winter. There was a cycle that occurred every forty-seven years. It dropped the whole planet into winter conditions for half the year rather than the usual quarter that happened on only half the planet at a time. The long period between the big winters, based on the reports Imara had read, lulled the citizens into a sense of security until the freeze was upon them. Apparently, they also forgot that the whole planet froze.

It didn't help that the smaller population that self-identified as the Rhone had chosen this year to revolt against the larger population that identified themselves as Serdobans. The animosity that had been festering for a century suddenly and inexplicably exploded along with munitions lobbed by the Rhone militia. Munitions that no one on the Serdoban side was even aware of the Rhone possessing.

Now, not only were the people of Abira dealing with diminished food supplies, they had a civil war in their laps, too.

That was part of the reason the Hospitallers were here. The Hospitallers had been asked for as mediators by both sides. They'd also been asked to help with food aid. The armies on both sides were in standdown mode while Hospitaller dropships brought food to the towns and cities in the direst of need. They still had four months before the first thaw began.

"Sgt Fermo?" Cpl Bowers had moved up to stand beside Imara.

She indicated a direction several degrees off of north. "Company's coming."

02

First platoon's crawlers were closest to the approaching cloud of snow being kicked up a kilometer away. The company CO, Maj John Stewart, along with XO, Capt Leon McBride, Lt White, Lt Sheldon Neal of second platoon, and 1stSgt Nelson Dawson, crossed the snow-blanketed field to meet the short convoy that continued to approach.

"Think they're glad to see us?" Cpl Bowers asked Imara.

Occasionally the Hospitallers weren't looked on with favor or relief. Sometimes, prior experiences with other forces poisoned a people's appreciation. That made it difficult for the Hospitallers to show that not all visiting forces came with violence as their priority. Rarely were the Hospitallers unsuccessful in winning hearts and minds.

"I think," Imara said as she watched several oversized snowmobiles separate themselves from the roiling cloud of snow they were throwing into the air, "that they'll be glad to see the supplies."

The snowmobiles were large, with two sets of tracks on both sides. Each of them had a driver and guard, dressed for the weather, and barely protected behind the windshield. The backs of the vehicles held small, covered, truck beds. Imara supposed that the dignitaries they would be working with were somewhat safe inside the covered beds. She was pretty sure they were about as comfortable as an Orphan Corps private on their first trip planetside in a dropship.

"We going to be able to hear anything from here?" asked Cpl Larson, who had crunched his way over to where Imara and Bowers were standing.

"If they're related to Cummings," said Cpl Bowers, "we'll hear everything."

"I heard that," Cummings said loud enough that the next squad over, Sgt Stacy Delgado's squad, laughed.

"Sound carries over the snow," Imara said. It was a warning to her squad. Watch what you say, the civilians might hear. Not that she was concerned her people might say something inappropriate, but that the civilians might decide to hear it as inappropriate. She pointed with her chin in the direction of Maj Stewart's party and the slowing snowmobiles. "Here we go."

Imara's comm beeped. She tapped it while watching the snowmobiles pull a U-turn and then stop. "Go ahead."

"Hey, Fermo."

"Hey, Delgado."

"If you hear anything good, have Cummings repeat it."

Imara chuckled. "Right. I'll let you know what I know."

Soon enough, they'd know all they'd needed to know. Maj Stewart would pass along all the information the company would need to do their jobs. No one was left in the dark. That was the Hospitaller way.

Out across the snow, doors were opening on the backs of the snowmobile beds. Several people in thick, quilted long coats stepped out. One of them pushed their way past the others and bent at the waist, vomiting whatever meal they'd eaten onto the snow.

"Ew, gross." The voice was quiet and behind where Imara and the two fireteam leaders stood.

"Pfc Harmon, shush," Imara said.

"She's right," said Cpl Larson.

Imara did not reply. She watched as the motion sick civilian wiped at their mouth with their sleeve while kicking snow over where they'd puked. The civilian looked around and stopped moving when their gaze passed over where Imara and the other Hospitallers were standing. They offered a brief wave and then high-stepped through the snow, joining the other civilians and the Hospitaller leadership.

Behind her, Imara couldn't fail to hear several of her people chuckling.

Despite how well noise traveled across the snow, Imara heard only unintelligible sounds from the two conferring groups. Likely it was nothing more than banal greetings that dragged on, slowing down the process of logistics. They needed to know where to take the crawlers. They needed to know how the civilians wanted to handle the distribution of supplies. Most communities left that to the Hospitallers. After all, this was what they did for a living. But there were always those few who felt it necessary to assert dominance by controlling what the Hospitallers could do, where they could do it, and when. The standard response among Hospitallers was to mentally shrug and then cooperate with the civilians to the best of their ability.

Every once in a while, someone attempted to use the distribution of supplies as a form of strong-arm control over a community. Though the Hospitallers avoided interfering with internal politics, they weren't going to let anyone starve just so someone could puff themselves up. Everyone would be treated equally. If they weren't, the Hospitallers would make sure it happened.

"That was quick." Imara was surprised to see the two parties moving away from each other.

"It's too cold for niceties," Bowers said. "Even they aren't used to this weather."

"Politicians always make time for niceties," said Cpl Larson.

"Not real politicians," Imara said. Her comm beeped. "Sgt Fermo."

"Fermo, stand by." It was Capt McBride, the XO. "Waiting for the others."

Imara signaled for her fireteam leaders to return to their crawlers. They nodded silently and walked by while Imara stood alone, waiting for the other squad leaders to check in.

"They have a warehouse for us," Capt McBride said after the last squad leader had responded on the comm. "Coordinates coming to your HUD now. It's going to be a tight fit. There used to be two warehouses, but one of them was destroyed recently."

"Destroyed?" Imara had meant to think the question rather than spit it out. "Sorry, Capt McBride."

"No problem, Fermo. We'll get you all updated once we're out of the weather."

"Weather?" asked another squad leader. It was either Johnson or Patterson. Their voices always sounded the same over the comm, even if they looked nothing alike.

"Storm's rolling in. Look east. We have two hours to get everything inside. Once you have the coordinates up on your displays, we'll roll. Sgt Fermo, your squad has point."

"Copy that, Capt McBride."

Imara tapped the side of her helmet, waking the HUD. On the left, she had a list of people on the comm. Top right, a message waited. She reached out and tapped the air beyond where she saw the message in the HUD. The message expanded, revealing coordinates that she then transferred to a map with several more hand gestures. She forwarded the map with its marked destination on to her fireteam leaders.

The map didn't need to stay open for Imara to find her way. This was part of the ability that Cpl Bower was amazed by the most. Once Imara had seen the location on the map, she'd find her way there. The others liked to have the map for reassurance and to check if Imara missed the designated location.

The company arrived ahead of the storm, though the snow was beginning to fall thicker from the sky. Imara hadn't relied on the HUD map and only needed her innate ability for the first half kilometer. The warehouse they'd been directed to was one of the tallest buildings near the town. It was also an easy hundred meters long. Imara wondered how something so large would be a tight fit for their twenty-four crawlers.

A giant roll-up door on one of the short ends of the building growled as it retracted, chains clanking like some ancient ghost of lore. The passage into the warehouse was wide enough for three of the crawlers to enter at once. Imara conferred with Lt White and the other squad leaders before directing the platoon's crawlers down the port side of the warehouse.

Inside, where it was ten or fifteen degrees warmer, Imara caught the smell of harvested grain. The floor held the telltale chaff that had been swirled into natural patterns by winds slipping under the doors.

The warehouse wasn't empty despite the lack of grain. The walls were lined with double rows of agricultural equipment. There were tens of tractors, cultivators, harvesters with long conveyor belts looking like giant, flat snakes rising over the vehicle cabs. Most of them looked well taken care of. But some, Imara noticed, looked damaged by fire, and others even had bullet holes, clearly having been in the way of some conflict or another.

Imara tapped her comm. "Lt White? Weren't we told that the civil war hadn't reached highland farmlands?"

"That's right," said Lt White. "You see something that suggests otherwise?"

"Bullet holes in some farming equipment. Not much rust, so it's likely recent. Smoke or fire damage on several others. Not the kind that indicates fire from the equipment."

"Fire damage, like from being inside a building destroyed by fire?" The lieutenant did not present a voice of surprise.

"The destroyed warehouse?" They'd passed it as they'd neared the warehouse they were now rolling into. The walls were mostly standing. The roof was gone, the roll-up doors somewhere on the ground, buried by the deepening snow.

"We were told it was a random fire," Lt White said. "Maj Stewart has his doubts, so let's keep that under wraps for now."

If she noticed the damage, Imara was sure other Hospitallers would notice as well. "I'll do my best, Lieutenant."

They both closed the comm at the same time. Imara turned and waved the first crawler to keep moving. With all the farming equipment already stowed inside the building, it truly was going to be a tight fit. She followed along as the second crawler passed. They made their way, guided by Pfc Harmon and Pfc Cummings until they were several meters shy of the far end of the building. Here there was another wide roll-up door. Imara noticed there were several other doors along the length of the building that were sized for humans and not their farm equipment.

Several civilians stood by one door, their long, quilted coats hanging open, revealing thick trousers and long, heavy-looking shirts. Imara nodded and received one in return before the civilians turned their backs to her and bent their heads toward each other in conversation.

"Hey, Sarge," Cpl Bowers said. She'd come up behind Imara, who was just turning away from the civilians. "Can I ask you something?"

"Is it about the bullet holes and scorch marks?"

Bowers laughed. "I thought you were only good at directions, not reading minds."

Imara responded with a grin before saying, "If that was going to be the subject of your question, the answer is don't ask. Not for now."

"Got it," said Cpl Bowers. "Should we start unloading?"

"That's a good question. I don't have an answer. Not yet. Have everyone stand by."

Imara made her way down the row of crawlers. The fit wasn't as tight as she'd initially thought. They could have easily fit another eight crawlers. She nodded to Sgt Delgado, who fell in alongside her. They continued until they reached Lt White, standing with SSgt Cedric Brewer, Sgt Zimmerman, and Capt McBride.

They both saluted as they approached. "Capt McBride. Lt White," Imara said.

"Fermo, Delgado," said Capt McBride as he and white returned the salute. "Glad you found your way here."

"How are things up front?" Lt White asked.

"Good," answered Imara. "There are a couple civilians by the doors up there. And plenty of farm equipment."

"About that," said Capt McBride. "The leadership of Bhisho swear there hasn't been any action up in this valley. The evidence suggests otherwise. So, we'll honor their lie, but prepare for surprises."

"Got it," Imara said. Next to her, Sgt Delgado nodded in agreement.

"Now, the supplies." Capt McBride looked at Lt White.

"We have a rough schematic of where to put everything," Lt White said. She had her tablet in her hand and was tapping the screen. I've sent all the NCOs the floorplan and the distribution pattern. We'll get it all on the ground so we can pull the crawlers out in the morning. Supplying the people of Bhisho will begin at that time. Questions?"

As no one had any, the NCOs saluted the officers and returned to their crawlers.

"It's not a race," Imara said over the comm once she was connected to her squad. "So don't do anything foolish."

She could hear the snickering around her. They were gonna race no matter what. Well, it was a healthy competition, and the losers only had to deal with a few hours of good-natured ribbing.

The competition also made short work of the job. It was another hour before most of the supplies were off the crawlers and stacked in open places. Throughout the warehouse, Imara could see that the other squads were also not making a competition of the job.

"Hey, Cpl Larson," she said. When Larson looked her way, she pointed across the warehouse where second platoon was unloading. "Didn't you lose the last race to Cpl Riley?"

Larson shaded his eyes and looked where Imara had pointed. She could see him sag with a groan before he turned and began urging his fireteam to move faster. Larson and Riley were from the same year at the same orphanage. They were as much like brothers as two orphans raised together could be. That meant there was always some sort of competition between them.

Imara was about to suggest a way to get the last of the toiletries to their proper staging location when someone shouted 'attention,' and everyone went rigid. She followed suit.

"Maj Stewart," she said. The salute was returned by the major who was in the company of 1stSgt Dawson and Lt White.

"Fermo," said the major. "Tell your people to continue while we talk."

"You heard the major," Imara barked. She knew they heard because they were already moving. Still, she added, "Back to work."

A ragged volley of, "Yes, Sergeant," echoed back at her.

"Sgt Fermo," the major said once the troops were back to unloading and looking like they weren't trying to eavesdrop. "The locals insist we stay in the central gymnasium that they've prepared for us to bunk in."

"That doesn't seem like a good idea," Imara said. She was visualizing the bullet holes in the farm equipment.

"Agreed. But we also like to keep the local leadership on our side. So, we'll be using the gymnasium as company headquarters but keeping a guard here at the warehouse. The civilians don't like it, but they're smart enough not to push too hard."

"And my squad has first watch," said Imara. Why else come and speak to her directly.

Maj Stewart grinned. "Thank you for volunteering, Sgt Fermo."

03

Imara stood in VR, watching the snowstorm whipping the air with sheets of small, hard snowflakes. Using one hand, she shifted the image along, letting the world slide past her. The few lights of the town that were visible stabbed through the darkness like swords made of light, battling snow flurries.

"Beats actually being out there," said Cpl Larson.

Larson was standing next to Imara. Though she couldn't see him, she knew he was an arm's length away, piggybacking on her VR. He couldn't control the scene and had to deal with the occasional vertigo that came with being a passenger.

"Yes, it does," Imara said. She pulled on the virtual controls, turning them and making the world rotate slowly around her. She was now looking along the other side of the warehouse. "The signals look good."

"Someone had the bright idea to pair the eyes with hands for signal amplification."

"Thank you," Imara said. It was her idea, but only because she was in charge of the squad.

Eyes and hands were proprietary equipment also designed by the Hospitaller R&D facilities. Eyes were spheres capable of capturing three hundred sixty degree images. If enough eyes were on, capturing the same data, it was possible to create a 3D world to walk through in VR. Hands were self-propelled, four-legged walkers that could listen, sample the atmosphere, water, and ground, and a host of other things that required accessing the manual to learn about them. They were referred to as hands because they looked like a hand with a cleanly severed stump. The middle finger was the sensor. The stump was the antennae, computer, and power source.

When an eye and hand were combined, they were great for infiltrating a location, or for security. Tonight, the squad had done a great job setting them out. It would be a one-person affair with Hospitallers trading off every thirty minutes until second squad came out to relieve them.

"Where's Pvt Rodriguez?" Imara asked.

"Coming, Sarge," answered Rodriguez. Imara could hear but not see his boots as he trotted over. "Pvt Rodriguez reporting."

Imara tapped a virtual button that dropped her out of VR. She closed her eyes and took a breath until the moment of dizziness passed. When she opened them, she nodded to Rodriguez. "You have first watch. You have any doubts, let me or Cpl Larson know, A.S.A.P."

"Will do, Sgt Fermo." Rodriguez tapped his helmet, lowering his face shield and then tapped it again, waking his VR system. Imara watched his head and hands move until he responded. "I'm in."

"Keep a sharp eye," Imara said. She left him and Cpl Larson, making her way to a table that had been set up between the farm equipment and the second crawler.

Pfc Sullivan had taken it upon himself to fix up some rations for everyone to eat. They had chili, reconstituted fruit, and Insta. They'd have to wait until they were back on the ship to get actual coffee. Until then, it was the Hospitallers' best friend, Insta, for everyone.

Smelling the food reminded Imara that she was hungry and that she needed to eat something. She filled a bowl with chili before stepping over Pfc Cummings's legs to reach the urn of hot Insta. After filling a metal cup with the steaming brew, she made her way over to a tractor tire, lying on its side.

"Could have used that Insta a few hours ago," said Cpl Bower as she scooted sideways, creating room for Imara.

"Truth to that." Imara set the cup down before scooping up several spoonfuls of the chili. She chewed on it slowly as she thought about the end of the day. After washing down the chili with Insta, she said, "Not sure why the people of Bhisho want to deny an attack having occurred."

The comment was meant for the air and not really in need of a response. However, as Bower was sitting next to her, it made sense that the corporal would answer.

"Maybe they're embarrassed that they lost all of their food and an important building? Maybe they were the original aggressors and this was payback? They don't want to admit that for fear we'll pull our supplies and go away?"

Imara nodded. "Right, there are lots of reasons. You should rest, Corporal. Your fireteam has the second half of the shift."

"What about you, Sgt Fermo? You have to rest, too."

"You don't get to rest when you're on the shortlist for staff sergeant." She grinned. "Didn't you know that once you get that promotion, your body never needs sleep again."

Cpl Bower's disbelief came as a snort. "Right, Sarge. But you aren't a staff sergeant yet, so do try and rest some."

"I will," Imara said. She lifted her cup. "Just as soon as I have three or four of these."

Bowers waved Imara off, including a disbelieving shake of her head. She walked over to the first crawler where Pfc Harmon was already stretched out, hands laced together across her abdomen. Likely not asleep, but at least resting.

Imara looked behind her. Cummings, on the other hand, could sleep anywhere, anytime. It was a skill that Imara envied. It wasn't that she didn't like to sleep. She used to enjoy it. When she'd had company, sleep had been nearly euphoric. The thought brought her hand to her pocket. The two pocket knives were together in parallel. A part of them was still in contact, even if Imara couldn't be. She breathed deeply several times, letting the pain wash over her and then slip away for the time being. It had been a year, but it was still hard to let go.

The chili had gone cold in the bowl. Easily done in the cold warehouse. Imara ate it anyway. No need to let it go to waste. Not on a world where supplies had reached a critical point. Forty-seven years to plan and yet humans still managed to ignore the obvious. Fortunately for the people of Abira, the Hospitallers had learned several centuries ago to prepare for the worst and never forgot that lesson. So, when the call came from the planetary government, begging for help with the cease-fire and food, the Hospitallers were there in weeks, having pulled in supplies from across the radial arm.

Now the Insta had gone cold. Imara quaffed the last of what was in her cup before pouring more of the hot stuff from the tall urn. She drank it while standing at the table, her eyes staring beyond the confines of the warehouse. Her thoughts pulled her along until someone tapped her shoulder. She blinked and looked around.

"Pvt Rodriguez. Your VR shift over already?"

"Yes, Sergeant."

She stepped back and waved at the table. "Well, grab a bite and then get some sleep."

"I'd like to, but Cpl Larson said to come and get you."

"All right." Imara put her cup on the table. "I'll go. You eat. That's an order, and I outrank Cpl Larson."

Rodriguez grinned. "It's not my job to question orders." He grabbed a bowl and dug into the chili with the ladle.

On the other side of the crawlers, Cpl Larson was standing next to Pfc Carol Walters. Both of them looked like statues. Except for their hands. They were both moving them in a way that indicated both of them were in VR.

Imara tapped her comm. "Larson? What's going on?"

"Not sure," Larson said through the comm. His voice was quiet, slow, like he was focused elsewhere. "But I think we might have company."

"In this weather?" If it had been closer to the end of their shift, Imara might have assumed it was Sgt Delgado and her squad. But even then, Delgado would have communicated her presence rather than sneak over. "What direction, Cpl Larson?"

"South. Five bodies. I think."

"Stand by. I'm coming in." Imara brought down her face shield and tapped into the VR.

She blinked twice in confusion. Everything was dark blue when it should have been black with swirls and drifts of snow. Unless Larson and Walters were using one of the other wavelengths. She tapped one of the virtual buttons at the bottom of her vision and opened the details. Yes, they were in thermal.

"Where are you looking?" she asked.

"Here," said Pfc Walters.

A rough circle seemed to draw itself in the air in front of Imara. She studied the space inside the circle until she finally saw the signals. There were five, very faint red ovals that occasionally winked out of existence or narrowed and then expanded once more. Snow swirls or looking down at the ground would make the signal disappear. Turning left or right would narrow them. Imara's first thought was that the approaching figures were wearing thermal masking uniforms. But that was high tech. The other option could be that they were heavily bundled and been outside so long that their outer layers now matched the temperature of the air around them.

"Good eye, Walters. Larson. Dropping out." Imara closed her eyes and took several breaths as she exited VR.

Who would come from the south? And why only five? Definitely not Delgado. Imara tapped her comm, connecting with her squad. "On your feet people, we may have company. Someone make sure Cummings wakes up quietly."

"I'm awake, Sarge." Cummings's voice came as a whisper.

"Pull back from any door you might be near," Imara said. "Wait for further instructions."

Along the edges of the crawlers, Imara saw several of her people moving into protective positions. She tapped the comm again, connecting with Cpl Larson. "Update me."

"They're definitely coming here," said Larson. "Thermal's improved as they've gotten closer. They're keeping to the shadows and avoiding the light spilling over from the rest of the town."

"West side of the building?" She had more people and could afford to split them up. Over the comm and by proximity, Imara heard Pfc Schultz laugh. "What's funny? We could all use a laugh."

"Sorry, Sgt Fermo," Schultz said. "It's just that they don't seem to be very good at this. Most of them anyway. There's no sound, but it seems like one of them keeps stopping to bark commands at the others. It reminded me of basic training."

"Amateurs? Well, that'll make this a bit easier." Trained military would have been the likely assumption and almost a surprise. If the leaders of Bhisho were willing to deny their warehouse being lost in an attack, they might also not want to admit soldiers were in the area. Likely out of fear of having the supplies delayed in their arrival.

"Sergeant? They crossed over and are now along the wall of the warehouse. About halfway along."

Imara grinned and tapped the comm to pull her entire squad into the conversation. "Let's have some fun."

Imara's squad was well trained, unlike the people struggling with the locks on the warehouse door. Cummings had offered to sneak over and turn at least one of the two locks to make it easier. It was a humorous idea, but Imara had to decline. Still, she was worried that Sgt Delgado would come along before the intruders could get inside, scaring them away. Then, not only would Imara's squad not have the fun of capturing them, they wouldn't learn anything about their intentions or where they came from.

"Here we go," Cpl Bowers whispered into the comm.

The hushed grating sound of a door slowly being pulled open was accented by a burst of cold air. Imara felt it from halfway across the warehouse, where she was sitting on several boxes of dehydrated stew. A whispered voice was quickly followed by a harsh shush. The door scraped closed, and the winter breeze hurtling through the building evaporated.

Imara couldn't see the intruders, but she knew where her own people were. She knew that as the intruders moved further into the warehouse, her people would close in behind. The Hospitallers were creating a box that would move with intruders, ready to collapse in on them when the signal was given.

Though they still knew nothing about the intruders, Imara was certain their presence was related to the Hospitallers appearing with twenty-four crawlers laden with food supplies. Where they came from was still the mystery. Where they were going was marked by eight green dots on Imara's HUD. Those were her people. Except for Pfc Cummings on VR watch, they were all moving in her direction.

"I told you no one was here," said a voice in a harsh whisper.

"You could not have known that while we were outside," a second voice said. This one's accent seemed different than the other.

They had crossed the line of crawlers and were on the edge of open space between them and the supplies.

"They invited all of the orphan trash to the gymnasium. You said so." A third voice, a similar accent to the first voice.

"Never underestimate a Hospitaller," said the accented voice.

"Look at all that food," another voice said. They sounded eager. "Can we just take some? They can't actually know if something is missing."

"We need to report back. Maybe you'll get some of it later."

"Come on, Dmytro, just a case. We can eat it along the way."

"No, you can't," Imara said. There were several yelps of surprise as she spoke. "You didn't even say please."

The other Hospitallers stepped out of hiding. Their helmet task lights came on, illuminating the group of intruders. They were dressed in double layers of the long quilted coats the people of Bhisho wore. They had thick hats pulled down over their heads, leaving only the small space between eyebrows and lower lip exposed. Four of the five looked scared. The fifth one looked annoyed. Imara directed her question at him. "Where are you from?"

"None of your business, Hospitaller," he said. The accent marked him as the one referred to as Dmytro. Imara noted the lack of concern in his voice.

Fortunately, the other four didn't seem as resilient. One of them answered before Dmytro could silence any of them.

"Grabouw. We're from Grabouw."

"Next valley? That's eleven and a half kilometers away."

"Yes," said another of the intruders.

"Shut up!" barked Dmytro.

"We don't have any food," one of them said and then shied away from Dmytro's glare.

"Well, you've come to the right place," Imara said. "And the wrong place."

04

None of the intruders, now confirmed as civilians from the neighboring town of Grabouw, carried any weapons. Not even the cranky Dmytro. Once they'd all been searched, Imara guided them to the table with the food Pfc Sullivan had laid out earlier. She sat them down and invited them to eat while she contacted Lt White on the comm.

By the time Lt White arrived with Sgt Delgado's squad, Maj Stewart, and 1stSgt Dawson, four of the five civilians from Grabouw were well fed. They'd shed their outer coats and had the undercoat unbuttoned and hanging open. They appeared content with their situation.

Dmytro appeared less so.

He rose as Maj Stewart entered the area around the table as marked by Imara's squad, who seemed amused by the situation. Something she felt herself. The Grabouwians had come a long way, through a snowstorm, to find food. And only one of them seemed upset about their present situation.

"You cannot detain us," he said. "We are non-combatants."

Maj Stewart paused, his head tilted to one side several centimeters. He slowly smiled and then looked around. "Is that Insta I smell?"

"Yes, Major," Pfc Sullivan said. "Would you like a cup?"

"Definitely. They don't drink it here on Abira. Nor coffee, it seems."

"We like green tea," said one of the civilians at the table. "Though I could get used to this Insta."

"Hush," said Dmytro.

"All right, let's keep this civil. Insta for everyone, Pfc Sullivan, if you don't mind?"

"My pleasure, Maj Stewart."

Maj Stewart, with Lt White and the first sergeant shadowing him, sat at one end of the table. He politely accepted his cup of Insta from Sullivan. He then waited until everyone, including Delgado's squad, had a cup in their hand. Imara found it comical but kept her amusement to a small smile. The major looked her way once and responded to Imara's smile with a single raised eyebrow.

After several sips that brought a different smile to Maj Stewart's face, he began to ask questions.

"So, you are all from Grabouw?"

"We don't have to answer," said Dmytro.

"Yes," said one of the others.

"Really? All of you?"

Imara noted the downward casting of eyes from four of them. Only Dmytro seemed willing to look Maj Stewart in the eyes.

"Yes, we are," Dmytro said.

"Right, right." Maj Stewart paused for a couple more sips from his cup of Insta.

Coffee was plentiful but not always available. Long before they had a steady supply of coffee beans, the Hospitaller organization developed its synthetic version, an instant version. And while it was hot and soothing, it had its own unique flavor that no one would ever mistake for coffee. Every Hospitaller had been drinking it since their teenage years at the orphanages. It was almost like a rite of passage, similar to the receiving of the pocket knife.

"So," the major said after setting his cup on the table. "You were all just out for a walk? Snowstorm kicked up, and you dodged in here to escape the weather?"

The four remained silent.

"Yes," Dmytro said. "Something like that."

"And everything in Grabouw is well?"

"Yes."

"No."

Imara watched as Maj Stewart and Dmytro turned their attention to the civilian who had contradicted Dmytro's answer.

"Who are you?" Maj Stewart asked.

The man looked at Dmytro and then at the major. "Ervik Baker. I am part of the town council for Grabouw."

Ervik Baker also looked older than the other men present, including Dmytro.

"And everything is not well in Grabouw, Mr. Baker?"

"It is not. Our town hungers, too. And yet you bring food here only. Because they are Serdobans, and we are Rhone."

The major leaned toward Ervik Baker, resting one forearm on the table between them. "We brought food to the town of Bhisho because the central government asked us to."

"The central government can go spit," said one of the other men. "They only care for the Serdobans. They care nothing for Rhone. It has always been that way."

Imara was sure that wasn't the case. She'd read the history brief when it was sent to her tablet. The world had been at peace for nearly as long as it had been settled. True, the Rhone were the minority population, but they also had equal representation on the central council and shared roles as President and Prime Minister.

What hadn't been clarified in the brief was why there was a sudden and violent civil war initiated by the Rhone. Nor how they'd managed to acquire some very modern equipment with which to wage their war.

"I know nothing about that," said Maj Stewart in response to the other man's complaint. "We don't play sides when it comes to providing aid."

"Lies! Everyone knows the Hospitaller only help those they can then control."

The man shrunk in his chair as every Hospitaller around him took a step forward. Imara was surprised to see that she had been doing the same thing. She stepped back and signaled for her squad to do the same. Sgt Delgado mimicked the action, drawing her people back, too.

"You would be?" Maj Stewart let the question hang.

The man hesitated, his gaze shifting to the others at the table. Then, in a voice meeker than his previous proclamation, he answered. "Bryant. Kaloyan Bryant. I'm also on the town council."

"Mr. Bryant, I'm not sure where you get your information from, but it is incorrect. Our motto is, aid, comfort, defend. That is what we are here for. To provide aid."

"Only to the Serdobans." Kaloyan Bryant folded his arms across his chest and sat back in his chair.

"To anyone that needs it."

"We need it," said Ervik Baker. "We have no food, either."

"And we will be glad to assist you," the major said. "But you can't just come here and steal it."

"We weren't going to steal it."

"Shut your hole, Ervik." Dmytro had risen from his chair. He seemed ready to launch across the table if it weren't for the sudden presence of Cpl Larson's hand on his shoulder. As he slowly sat, he added, "You've said enough. No more."

Ervik Baker looked more than nervous to Imara. He looked frightened. What was Dmytro Barnes's role in Grabouw?

"Doesn't matter now." Maj Stewart dismissed the outburst with a wave of one hand. "We'll be happy to send some of the supplies over to Grabouw in the morning."

"We can take them ourselves," Dmytro said. He wasn't looking at the major. Rather, he was glaring at the other four men at the table. None of them were returning his gaze.

"You probably could," Maj Stewart said. "But that's not how we do it. I'll send a squad with you to transport four crawlers of supplies and see to their distribution."

"Four? There are more than twenty of them right here." Kaloyan Bryant was up and pointing as if the Hospitallers hadn't noticed the number of crawlers present.

"There are. But you don't need all or even half. Tomorrow, while we send you home with four crawlers of supplies, I will make contact with my commander and arrange for additional supplies for Grabouw and Bhisho. It'll take a few days to get the supplies ready, but with four crawlers full, you'll manage at least a month."

"It's not fair," Kaloyan said as he slumped into his chair.

Maj Stewart stood. "Fair or not, Mr. Bryant, that's what I can do. If you'd like to return to Grabouw empty-handed...?"

"We'll take it," Dmytro said. His words snapped like dry sticks as he spoke them. "That will be plenty."

"No, it won't." Kaloyan's words were muttered, and Imara wondered if anyone else had heard him.

"My people will give you some blankets and a relatively comfortable spot to spend the night. You'll be under guard, though. I'm sure you'll understand. Lt White? Please take care of that."

"Yes, Major." Lt White waved Sgt Delgado over.

The major turned and scanned the people around him. His scan stopped when it crossed Imara. She had a sudden flutter in her stomach.

"Sgt Fermo. Make sure your people get some rest. I want you all bright-eyed and bushy-tailed come sun up."

"Did we just volunteer for the convoy, Major?"

Maj Stewart grinned. "Yes, you did."

Imara and the rest of her squad arrived back at the warehouse shortly after the sun had risen, stomping new snow off their boots. The gymnasium that had become their temporary headquarters was roomy and even had a small kitchen. Everyone in the squad, including Imara, had dropped onto bunks the moment they'd arrived and fallen asleep in minutes.

Only once in the night had Imara woken, driven there by a dream she didn't want to have. She'd brushed her hand across the pocket with the two small knives pressed against each other before drifting asleep once more.

Imara's tablet had beeped her awake a short time later and fifteen minutes before the rest of the squad. She'd smelled the Insta from the kitchen moments before the beeping began. As was usual for the rest of the squad, they'd begun to stir even as she'd been strapping her boots to her feet. By the time she'd had her armor cinched in place, most of the others had been sitting or started to get dressed. The only bunk she'd had to kick was Cummings's and he was up the moment she did.

Before they'd all dropped for the night, she'd explained their new mission. None of them complained, but there was a sense of wariness.

"I don't think these Rhone people like us," Pvt Rodriguez had said.

Several others had muttered in agreement. Imara agreed, too, but she kept that to herself. None of them would disobey the orders or become a problem for the squad. They always followed their orders. They might not like them, but they followed them. And they trusted the officers and staff NCOs to look out for their best interest. Imara did not think that Maj Stewart would send them somewhere that he didn't think they could handle.

They entered the warehouse and found the four crawlers being assigned to them nearly finished with loading. Sgt Carlos Johnson and Sgt Aubrey Warren had been working with their squads since before dawn. The company XO, Capt McBride, had written up a pick-list of supplies, and the two squads had spent hours digging through the stacks on the warehouse floor to assemble the order.

"Well, maybe this won't be so bad," said Cpl Bowers as she stopped next to Imara.

They'd all been blinking the brightness of the outdoors away so they could see inside the warehouse that was half as bright at best.

"You're just glad we didn't have to do all the heavy lifting," Imara said. She gave a wave to Sgt Johnson, who waved back.

"Who do you think is going to unload it all, Bowers?" Cpl Larson had joined them as he asked his rhetorical question.

"Right, but then I'll be bored and dying for something to do."

"Hey, Fermo," said the approaching Sgt Johnson. "Hope you won't be disappointed. Sun chairs and umbrellas weren't on the list."

"That kills all the fun." Imara shook hands with Johnson. "Thanks for loading it all."

Johnson laughed. "To be fair, I'd rather load them than walk twelve kliks in the snow and cold."

"And unpredictable snowstorms." Sgt Warren had joined the small group. "Can't forget the snowstorms. That should make things interesting."

"Well, good. I was worried about being bored," Cpl Bowers said. She'd made the comment under her breath, but still loud enough that those around her could hear and have a good laugh.

"Just keep the Insta warm until we return," said Imara. Then, seeing Capt McBride approaching, she said, "Hospitallers! Attention!"

All around her, she heard the sound of boot heels clapping together. She saluted the approaching XO, knowing that the others behind her were doing the same thing.

"Stand easy," said Capt McBride as he returned the salute. "Sgt Warren? Crawlers ready to go?"

"Loaded and synced," Warren said.

Rather than having one controller for each of the crawlers, they were electronically chained to each other. Only one controller was needed along the way to Grabouw. Each of the following crawlers would trace the exact same path as the lead crawler. Once in the town, Imara would distribute the crawlers to different drivers.

"Now, all you need, Sgt Fermo, is a group of civilians to escort home." Capt McBride's face tightened as he mentioned the civilians from Grabouw. It seemed likely he felt the same way about the situation as the major and every other Hospitaller who had been present the night before.

Sgt Warren turned, cupped her hands around her mouth, and bellowed across the warehouse space. "Cpl Parsons! Bring them up."

"Yes, Sergeant."

Several seconds later, Cpl Parsons appeared with the five civilians. They looked rested and well fed. Dmytro still had a scowl on his face as he walked with the others. Imara also noticed that the other four kept some small distance between them and Dmytro as if he had something they might catch.

"Everyone ready to go?" Capt McBride asked. The question was for the civilians as the XO didn't have to wonder about Imara's squad. They were ready minutes after they'd woken.

"We don't need your people," said Dmytro. "I'm sure we can move the tractors just fine on our own."

"You might," said Capt McBride. "If they were your equipment. But they aren't. And until the supplies are officially handed over, they, too, don't belong to you. Now, if you would like to return empty-handed, that's fine with me. I'm not the CO, I don't have to play nice."

It didn't hurt that the XO was taller than the five civilians.

Ervik Baker stepped ahead of Dmytro. "We'll be glad to have your soldiers along," he said. "But, I would request that they return here as quickly as possible."

Capt McBride looked at Imara, Dmytro, and then down to Ervik Baker. "I don't think you'll get any argument from them."

Imara didn't respond, but she knew the captain was correct. Hospitallers, as a rule, didn't stay where they weren't wanted. The idea rubbed the wrong way against their motto of aid and comfort.

"Shall we proceed, then?" Ervik asked.

"By all means," the XO replied. He turned to Imara and said, "They're all yours, Sgt Fermo."

"Thank you, Captain." Imara turned and caught Pfc Cummings' attention. "Cummings, you're the first driver."

"On it, Sergeant." Cummings saluted Capt McBride and trotted up the line of crawlers to sync his system to the crawlers.

"Cpl Larson," Imara said. "Escort the civilians to the midpoint. Keep them company there. Let's move out."

Larson's fireteam waved for the civilians to proceed. Cpl Bowers lead the rest of her fireteam forward. Imara started to follow, but the sound of a throat being cleared stalled her progress.

"Captain?"

"Sgt Fermo. Maj Stewart's orders. Keep a sharp lookout. Report anything you see that's out of the ordinary. And watch your back."

"Will do."

Capt McBride smiled and returned Imara's salute. "Enjoy the walk, Sergeant."

05

As far as long walks went, Imara had to admit this one wasn't unpleasant. They'd all had to drop their face shields and adjust the light filters, the world around them was snow bright. The civilians had narrow wrap-around glasses with dark lenses that seemed to serve the same purpose.

There was a road that led a broad-arced path out of the Saastal valley and into the neighboring Mischabel valley. It was invisible, buried under a meter-plus of still accumulating snow. There was one river that connected the two valleys but was also hidden beneath the thick layer of snow. The pass between the two valleys was bracketed by forested slopes. The pine-like trees were sandwiched between snow at their roots and the caps of white that bowed their tops. They provided the only relief from the monochromatic white of either valley.

Just inside the Mischabel valley, Cpl Larson had pointed out a farmhouse near the eastern side of the pass.

"The civilians said it's deserted." A raised eyebrow telegraphed his feelings on that statement.

Imara had given the farmhouse a second glance, surprised by the information. There were small sections of the roof where the snow had melted away. There was some heat inside the building. And if there was heat, the place wasn't deserted. Another secret the people of Grabouw seemed determined to keep. The first chance she had, Imara would pass that information along to Maj Stewart.

For the moment, though, the Hospitallers let it pass just as they did the buried hedgerows and orchards.

At ten kilometers, the sun was long past its zenith. The shifting of shadows lifted the town of Grabouw from the white fields, hills, and sky. The streets of Grabouw, like those of Bhisho, had been plowed just enough to hint at their presence. In the piled snow to either side, Imara noticed openings that lead to narrow paths. The paths went directly to the front doors of the homes.

Imara noticed that the homes here were sharp-peaked and decorated with colorfully painted filigree dusted with snow. The window shutters were painted with colorful flowers. The doors were done in the same manner. Imara imagined that in the spring and summer, the town would look quite festive. There were probably even white picket fences hidden under the drifts of snow.

There were warehouses here in Grabouw, too. They were east and west of the town. More fields were supposed to be present on the south side of the valley, hidden by the town. A road in that direction also provided access to the lowlands. The brief Imara had read indicated that ground trains came in the fall to haul away the grains for sale across the planet and even to other nearby solar systems.

Imara thought that somewhere in that plan, they would have begun stashing a little more for themselves than other years until they built up a surplus. Likely, the price they were getting made it difficult to just sit on the grain.

Single homes gave way to row homes that stood back for business and government structures. These were planned towns, designed early in the planet's colonization, copied from other planets as they planned how people would live. Abira had also been an easy world to terraform, which was a valued trait in the early days of the second expansion.

In the center of Grabouw, just like Bhisho, there was a gymnasium. It was here that the civilians insisted the supplies should be stored.

"You don't want to put them in one of the warehouses?" Imara asked. "Wouldn't they be easier to manage?"

"We want them here." Dmytro, who seemed to have regained control of the group the further into town they got, jabbed the air in the direction of the gymnasium. "Is that so difficult to comprehend?"

At the edges of buildings, near the gymnasium and the four crawlers stacked tall with boxes and crates of food, more people were gathering. Imara hadn't been able to give them much more attention than a simple sweep of the area as she dealt with Dmytro. They seemed cautious, holding back, keeping curious children pressed against them.

"It's not difficult, Mr. Barnes. And since we're here, we might as well hand out a few meals to each of the people who are watching us."

"They can wait." Dmytro glared around him as if daring anyone to challenge him.

Imara had no problem doing just that. Without taking her eyes off of Dmytro, she called Cpl Bowers over.

"Yes, Sergeant?"

"I want everyone moving the supplies into the gymnasium. Sun's setting, so let's get this done."

"Will do, Sgt Fermo."

"Except you and Cummings." Imara still held Dmytro with her eyes. "Have Cummings pull down the emergency rations from the last crawler. Give three packets to each individual that steps up."

"I said they could wait," Dmytro said.

"The supplies aren't yours just yet, Mr. Barnes. Until then, the decision of what to do with them lies with me. If you'd like to complain to my CO, Pvt Gonzales can help you with a link."

"Sgt Fermo?"

"Yes, Bowers?" She watched as Dmytro chewed on words he might regret spitting out.

"We have a T-n-T crate back there, too."

A crate of T-n-T was not a box of explosives. It was a box of toys and treats, and no Hospitaller deployed anywhere in the second radial arm without a satchel stuffed with small toys and individually wrapped candies. What began centuries ago as a way to comfort children traumatized by war had become habit. It was one of the little joys the Hospitallers had on worlds filled with death, destruction, and war. Sometimes, Imara thought that it meant more to them than it did to the children they shared with.

"Yes," said Imara. The growing smile on Cpl Bowers's face revealed the truth of Imara's thoughts. "Crack that open, too."

"Listen, Hospitaller." Dmytro had stepped forward, putting a shoulder into the space between Imara and Cpl Bowers. "This is all fine. But why don't we get all the supplies into the gymnasium first, that way we can keep track of it all."

"Go, Bowers." Bowers nodded and turned away. Pfc Cummings caught up with her. Imara returned her attention to Dmytro. "We can keep track of it out here just as well, Mr. Barnes. Now, are any of the citizens of Grabouw going to help unload, or is it just my team?"

Dmytro turned and pointed at a new group of men who'd slowly approached. "You. Yes, all of you. Start unloading that last tractor and carry everything inside."

"Halt," said Imara. Her voice carried authority, and the men stopped. "We'll start with the first crawler. So we can better keep track of the supplies, as you'd desired, Mr. Barnes."

The work went a little faster than if the Hospitallers had done it all by themselves. The people of Grabouw were willing to help, but they looked about as hungry as the people over in Bhisho. They certainly looked more haggard. While Dmytro urged the people to work faster, Imara would pull one or two off the line and direct them to where Cpl Bowers and Pfc Cummings were still handing out emergency rations and small toys. They understood and hurried after a nod of thanks.

Many of them tore into the packages as soon as they received them. Most of the adults who weren't responsible for children returned to carrying supplies into the gymnasium once they'd eaten. They worked a little harder and with a brighter look in their eyes.

By the time it was dark, the crawlers were completely unloaded, the T-n-T crate was empty, and a snowstorm was picking up. Thick flurries of snow were pushed down the streets by bone-chilling winds, dampening Imara's enthusiasm. She'd hoped to return to Bhisho after unloading the crawlers. They could all huddle on top and rely on the data from the outbound travel to lead them back to the other town. If all else failed, they'd still have Imara's impeccable sense of direction.

The feelings of the people of Grabouw were mixed.

"Your machines can take you back, no problem," said Dmytro. "And I'm sure you wish to return as quickly as possible."

That was true. But Imara also wondered about this town. There was a wariness amongst the people that was more than just hunger and an underlying dislike for Hospitallers. The last made no sense. Hospitallers had never been to Abira prior to this request. So they'd never had a chance to make a bad impression.

"Look at the way the snow's moving," said another person. "That's just the beginning. It'll be whiteout conditions in a few hours."

"Their machines got fancy guidance stuff, Erig," said a woman. She was still holding several emergency rations in one hand, a well-bundled baby in another. One of the small terry cloth animals from the T-n-T crate peeked out from the bundle. "Just like our tractors. Maybe even better."

"Still no reason to make them go out in that kind of weather. What if one of them fell off?"

"They won't fall off," Dmytro said. "They'll be fine. That right, Hospitaller?"

"Whiteout conditions. Give them a place to stay the night."

Imara's comm buzzed. She surreptitiously tapped it while the argument continued.

Cpl Larson's voice whispered straight into her ear. "They really don't like us, do they, Sarge?"

Imara casually gave the signal for Larson to stand down. He wasn't wrong, but there wasn't any reason for the Hospitallers to get involved. Yet, there was a desire to understand more of the situation.

"Listen," Imara finally said. Her voice was just loud enough to cut through all the raised voices. "Stay or go, it's fine with us, but the snow is getting worse, and some of you have children in tow or waiting at home."

"Have the council vote," said the woman with the bundled baby.

"That's not necessary," Dmytro countered.

"It's what we do here," the man named Erig said. The emphasis made it clear that Dmytro wasn't from here.

Dmytro threw up his hands and walked away. Ervik Baker, Kaloyan Bryant, and four other people huddled together. Imara watched the snow settle on their shoulders. If they took too long, she reasoned, they'd be as buried in snow as the hedgerows that divided their fields.

Fortunately, they only had a shawl's depth of snow on them by the time they came to a conclusion.

"We think you should stay the night," Ervik Baker said. "There is a house a few blocks away. The family left when the fighting started. You can stay there until morning."

"Or until the storm dies down," added the woman. "Whatever feels safe to you."

Imara noticed that the woman's eyes shifted in Dmytro's direction as she finished talking.

"We'll be glad to accept your hospitality," said Imara.

Imara's squad followed Ervik and Kaloyan, who guided them down another street that led toward the western edge of the town. The few street lights that worked in this section of town illuminated the now heavily falling snow more than they did the street. The Hospitaller task lights weren't much better. Fortunately, Ervik knew where he was going, and no one had to rely on Imara's sense of direction. Not that it would have guided them to a building she'd never been to.

The first thing Imara noticed on the last street they'd turned on was the number of homes heavily blanketed in snow. Three on the west side of the street, two on the other. The road that passed between them was unmarked by any recent passage. The paths to the doorways were half blanketed in new snow.

"Why are these houses all empty?" ask Imara. As she spoke, she signaled to Cpl Bowers and Larson to drop several eyes along the way. They might get lost in the snow, but the thermal and infrared would still be useful.

"Serdobans," Ervik said. He shrugged then added, "They didn't feel like they belonged any more and chose to move elsewhere. I think some went to Bhisho. Others went elsewhere."

"The Meiers went to Bhisho," said Kaloyan. "The others went down to Rosendal before winter set in."

"Didn't feel like they belonged?" Imara asked. She had pulled one of the mechanical hands out of one of her uniform's pouches and was turning it on. The two men hadn't bothered to look in her direction while they spoke.

"Well, being Serdobans..." said Kaloyan. He let his words trail off as if Imara should be able to comprehend the rest of the statement. She could have, but it was unlikely that it would have been a response he would have liked.

Instead, she gently tossed the hand into the snow and signaled for several other members of her squad to do the same. Then she said, "And you all being Rhone?"

"Right." Ervik's response was curt. He no longer seemed comfortable with the conversation. He tapped Kaloyan, using the back of his hand, and then pointed to the middle house on the west side. "That house has the most rooms."

"Winzelers," added Kaloyan. "They were a big family. Operated a good orchard."

Imara wasn't sure if the use of past tense should be seen as ominous. Either way, she was about finished with trusting the leadership of Grabouw.

"This'll be fine, I guess."

"Door might be locked," Ervik said. He held out a hand. "Good night, Hospitaller. Thank you for what you've done."

Imara shook hands. Ervik pressed something into her palm, and she accepted it without expression, cupping it as their hands parted.

"Let's go, Kaloyan. I'm freezing."

They waved good-bye and quickly left the Hospitallers.

06

"They're right," Imara said as she watched them leave. "It is cold. Pfc Walters, check the doors, see if we can get in without doing damage. Sullivan, you go with her."

"On it," they both said. They had to wade through the snow to reach the house. Walters tripped over something and temporarily disappeared from sight. Sullivan laughed and quickly apologized as Walters hefted several handfuls of snow at his face.

"Play later," said Imara. She switched her attention to the street and the rest of her squad. "Thoughts?"

"They isolated us," Cpl Larson said. "Several reasons why that could be. None of them that I like."

"Nor do I." Imara opened her hand to reveal a military patch. Threads hung off it like cobwebs. Wherever it came from, it had not been removed delicately.

"What do you have, Sgt Fermo?" asked Cpl Bowers.

"Unit patch," said Imara. She held her hand out so the others could see it. The first snowflakes that landed on it, melted, darkening the colors. "Anyone recognize it?"

"Not really," said Cpl Larson. "It looks sort of familiar, but I'm not sure from where."

"Serdoban," Cpl Bowers said. "I remember seeing something like it in the briefs we had to read. Maybe he was letting you know where his loyalties lie?"

Snowflakes dusted the patch now. Imara wiped them off as she studied the patch for a few more heartbeats. "I'm not sure," she said. "He was very discreet about it. I don't think he wanted anyone else to know he'd given it to me."

"Could it be a warning?" asked Larson.

Imara slipped the patch into a pocket. "That's a good question,

Larson."

"I have a question," Pfc Cummings said.

Imara nodded. "Fire away, Cummings."

Cummings pointed through the dark, over the tops of the nearest homes and buildings. "Hard to see right now, but there's a home that way. Three stories. Stands alone. It's bristling with antennae and a disguised satellite link-up. Why would a small town need all that hardware?"

"How do you know it's disguised?" asked Pvt Rodriguez.

"It's standard issue," answered Cpl Bowers. "I saw it, too. It might not be a big deal, except it's not on a government building."

"Rhone listening post?" Larson asked.

"It's a lot of equipment for a listening post," said Cummings.

"I agree. There's a lot more than listening going on there," said Cpl Bowers.

"Noted," said Imara. "Anything else?"

"Besides the fact that the people looked afraid of that Dmytro fella and seemed to have some equal fear and distrust of us?"

"That was changing, Rodriguez," Cummings said. "The more food and treats we handed out, the more I think people were wondering if what they knew about us was correct. One of the parents said we were much nicer than they'd been told to expect."

"Maybe we could talk about all this inside?" Pfc Walters had appeared through the falling snow. She was pointing over her shoulder as she spoke.

"Good idea, Walters. Everyone, inside."

The front door was locked, but Walters and Sullivan had managed to jimmy open a window and then access the double doors on the back patio. There was an extended roof over the patio. It kept the snow from piling up in front of the doors, though the drifts were slowly laying claim to the bare flagstones.

Everyone shook off the snow that had collected on them before stepping into the dining room just inside the double doors. It was a tight fit as all of the furniture was still present. Imara moved further into the house, feeling like an intruder. Her task light illuminated more than just furniture. Family photographs still hung on the walls. Old style print books still occupied a small set of shelves.

"Cpl Larson," Imara said. "Take your fireteam and do a sweep of the other rooms. Check the closets and any drawers you encounter."

"You think people might be hiding in the drawers and under the beds?"

"No, I don't. Just check." She was pretty sure what she would find. This wasn't an unusual scenario. "Bowers, check the kitchen, see if there's a pantry. Check it, too."

"Will do." Bowers disappeared into the kitchen.

"Cummings, you think you can get a fire going in that fireplace?"

"Yes, Sergeant."

Imara tapped her helmet, waking the VR. "I'm going to take a look and listen. Don't let me trip."

Cummings laughed. "I won't let that happen, Sarge, I promise."

The VR came online. Imara reached out and manipulated the virtual controls. The world she was looking at was mostly dark gray. Most of the eyes were sunk in the snow. Several of them showed the falling snow that would soon bury them. However, IR and thermal showed a little more. The houses back down the street they'd come glowed with life. The streets appeared empty.

The hands detected only the pressure of the falling snow. Imara used that as the baseline. She set an alarm for any pressure more significant than that, like people sneaking toward the house they were now inside. She switched back to the eyes and set motion detectors. They'd be less reliable than the pressure sensors on the hands, but it never hurt to be a little paranoid. That was all she could do for now. With a turn of a virtual knob, she closed down the program. When she came out of the VR and pushed her shield up, Cpl Larson was standing several meters back, waiting for her to regain her equilibrium.

"What did you find?" Imara asked.

"Clothes, toys, papers." Larson shrugged, his hands turning palm up as he did. "It's like they just went out for a quick run to the store, and they'll be back any moment."

"Driven out," Imara said. Another thing she needed to report back. "They very likely had a choice to leave immediately, whenever the threat was made, or stay and risk physical harm. The one family, the Meiers? They may have had family in Bhisho. The others went where they could. Not the first time I've seen something like this."

"Well, there's no food," said Cpl Bowers as she returned to the living room. "Cupboards are bare. However, there's rotted stuff in the fridge. So maybe the neighbors raided this place once the family was gone."

"Or when they ran short of their own supplies," said Imara. Which raised another question. Who attacked Bhisho and stole their supplies? The people of Grabouw seemed to be in the same if not in worse condition. Where did all the food go? "I need to report in. Let's stick an eye in every window and then eat and rest. Pvt Rodriguez and I will take first watch."

While the other Hospitallers settled in and opened the ration bars they carried, Imara went into the kitchen and tapped the comm for Maj Stewart. There was a lot of static which she attributed to the weather. However, there was also a hum way down on the register.

Maj Stewart's voice, when he spoke, crackled. "Sgt Fermo? I hope you're not out in this weather."

"No, Major. The council gave us an abandoned house to stay the night in. Used to belong to a Serdoban family."

"Serdoban? That's telling." Imara turned her head even though it did nothing to improve the signal. "Is the squad holding up?"

"They are. We're being looked after. Really well."

The comm went quiet for a second, and then the hum disappeared.

"Are you still being looked after?" Maj Stewart asked.

The absence of the hum meant that the major had switched them over to a scrambled comm channel.

"We're good now, Major," Imara said. Then, "I don't think Mr. Dmytro Barnes is from here. He doesn't know the town's ways. Whoever he is, he is feared more than respected."

"Did you notice his accent?" asked the Major. "He's not from this region. I wonder if he's even from this planet."

If Dmytro was from another planet, that changed the dynamics of the current situation drastically.

"I'm thinking, Major, that we shouldn't stay here."

"There's quite a snow storm blowing out there, Fermo."

Imara looked at the kitchen window. The snow was falling fast enough that flakes looked like streaks. It would be piling fast. The longer she and her squad stayed in the house, the more difficult it would be to get away. But where to go?

"We're not far from the western slope of hills, Maj Stewart. There's plenty of trees. We get in there we might be able to shelter in place until morning."

"You think you can get there? I don't want you risking your lives for nothing."

"I think we're risking our lives by staying here."

"Then do what you must to keep your people safe."

"Will do, Major. I'll report in when I feel we are." Imara tapped the comm, closing the channel. She wondered briefly if anyone had been listening in before the major secured the line would now act. And if they did, what could they expect?

She wasn't willing to wait and find out.

"Wrap it up," Imara said as she came into the living room. "Finish what you're chewing, pocket the rest. C.S.M.O."

"Not really much of a shop to close," Cpl Larson said. He was closing the seal on his ration bar.

"You want us to fry the eye and hands?" asked Cpl Bowers.

The technology of the Hospitallers was guarded. Two centuries ago, they'd had to rely on the tech of other military forces and civilian contractors. That made them dependent on outside influences. Influences that tried on many occasions to direct the actions of the Hospitallers, even if those actions were counter to the Hospitaller philosophy.

Grand masters had worked tirelessly to free the Hospitallers of the dependence on outsiders that interfered with their goals. As the Hospitallers grew, they engineered more and more of their own equipment and goods. The industries they built for themselves spanned the spectrum from toilet paper to spaceships. Much of it was proprietary, like the eyes and hands.

To protect their proprietary equipment, it was all built with a self-destruct. Anything left unattended for a specified amount of time would overheat its electronics. They could also go into the programming and initiate the self-destruct at any time. There were explosive, too. Enough that they could be used as low yield grenades if needed.

What mattered most was that the technology did not fall into anyone else's hands.

"Yes, Bowers, gather what we can, and then fry the rest before we move out."

"Sgt Fermo," Cpl Larson said. "The crawlers? I don't think we can take them without raising suspicions."

"Disable them, Larson. Not permanently, but lock them down. Maybe we'll be able to get them back. Let me know when that's taken care of so we can leave."

"Where to, Sarge?" asked Pfc Cummings. "And should I put the fire out?"

"Leave the fire going," said Imara. "As a matter of fact, pop a couple glow sticks and leave them behind, too. We're going west, into the woods."

"Um, we might have to hurry or belay that, Sgt Fermo." Pvt Rodriguez was standing in the doorway to the dining area. His face shield was down with the telltale glow of VR along the edges.

"What do you have, Rodriguez?" Imara dropped her own shield, tagging along with Rodriguez in VR.

The scene shifted but was less dizzying because everything was a cold, pale gray. Then, slightly brighter, warmer blobs became present. There were only three.

"They're not moving," Imara said. "How long have you been watching them?"

"Noticed them about two minutes ago. I was playing with the thermal gain. When I maxed it out, this is what I discovered."

Imara tapped out of the VR. They were fortunate that the three people watching them were between the houses on the other side of the street. They likely didn't expect the Hospitallers to leave out the back and head for the woods. Not with the storm as active as it currently was.

"Have you scanned behind the house, too?"

"It's just those three, Sgt Fermo. Also, the variegated thermal pattern gives me the impression that they're armed."

"Thank you, Rodriguez. Fry everything and drop out. We need to move."

It took an hour to clear the town and reach the fields that separated Imara and her squad from the woods. There'd been two more streets between the home they'd started from and the edge of town. There were fences between some of them. As the drifts of snow were so high, they'd tunneled to the fences. They cut through under the snow, collapsing the tunnels once through to the other side.

Only one home they passed had lights on. A lone individual stood at a window. They were looking in the direction that Imara and her squad had come, apparently unaware the Hospitallers were passing through the backyard.

There'd been more lights on the other streets, too. But with the snow falling so thickly, if someone wasn't looking to see them, the Hospitallers may as well have been invisible. No one shouted after them, no one shot at them. The hands they dropped along the way did not record any movement or sounds other than the prolonged hush of the falling snow.

"We need to stay close," Imara said. They were all on one knee, their weapons ready as needed. "It makes us more vulnerable, but we also don't want to risk anyone losing their way."

"You want us to tie on?" ask Cpl Larson?

Like mountain climbers, a rope to keep them tethered to each other for safety. But in a firefight, it was a liability.

"I think with shield down and night vision activated, you should all be able to keep tabs on the person in front of you." Imara looked at all of them until she had a nod from each. "Good. I have point. Try to keep no more than one meter apart, no less than one arm's distance."

"Should have showered," Cummings said. He earned the laugh he was after.

Imara was glad he did. It lightened the tense mood.

"In that case," Imara replied. "You get to bring up the rear."

Cummings groaned as the others chuckled. Imara ended it all and gave the signal to move out. She led the way, pushing through the snow built up around them and into the storm.

Imara did not have her night vision on. Her shield was down, but that was to keep the snow and the cold off her face as much as possible. The truth was that just as she'd been able to identify north and Bhisho with her eyes closed, she knew where the forest was and could have reached it blindfolded.

Every few minutes, she tapped the comm, setting the channel to a low frequency so that it didn't travel far, and did a roll call. She needed to hear eight voices. Each time she did, she breathed a sigh of relief.

It was a long two hours, and it was close to midnight local time when the first tree bole separated itself from the swirling snowstorm. Imara touched it, grateful for its presence.

"Ten meters more," she said through the comm.

Ten meters more and they were shielded from most of the weather. Here, snow drifted down in small, lazy flurries. The bases of the trees were barely covered with snow. It made for a decent place to rest until morning.

"Um, Sgt Fermo," Cpl Bowers said. Her voice was a whisper Imara almost didn't hear. "I don't think we're alone."

07

Instantly, the squad went still, turning outward to create a defensive position. Imara signaled Bowers to identify where?

Bowers signaled back and then pointed northward, not quite along the treeline but slightly further in.

Imara wanted to know how many, but Bowers wasn't sure. When Bowers signaled the distance, Imara relaxed several degrees. She waved Bowers close.

"What did you see?" Imara's voice was the ghost of a whisper.

"Looked like a patrol," Bowers whispered back. "They were moving north, backs to us. I'm sure we weren't detected."

"Patrol? You mean a military patrol?"

Bowers nodded, yes. This was not good. Imara had been told, the whole unit had been told that the Rhone and Serdoban forces were in the lower valleys, pulled back from a temporary DMZ. But if there was a patrol up here, it meant there were likely even more soldiers in the area.

It would be a dereliction of duty to turn and go back the way they had come. Imara knew she needed to know what sort of forces were here. So much for finding safety in the forest. She tapped shoulders and brought everyone closer together. Every other person was facing outward but backed in close enough they could hear.

"I'm not sure if we can follow that patrol, but that's what we're going to try and do," Imara told them. "We need to put distance between each of us. Comms on, keep the volume as low as you can and still be able to hear. You see something, say something. I think that we would be best served if we can avoid contact. This isn't the best place for a firefight. Our backs are exposed. Everyone understand?"

Everyone nodded, and that was all Imara needed.

She tapped Pfc Sullivan on the shoulder. "You got point. Remember, we don't want contact."

"Got it, Sarge," Sullivan whispered. He adjusted the comm using the controls on his chest and then lifted his shield. "I'll do better with natural sight."

"I think we all might," Imara said. "Get going. Bowers, you're next, then your fireteam. Larson, put someone on the backend and let's get going."

Sullivan started moving. He was a gray shadow in a gray world. Behind him, Pfc Harmon followed with Cpl Bowers moving shortly after. Once all of Bowers's fire team was in motion, Imara went. They moved slowly, stepping into the ever-widening indentations first created by Pfc Sullivan.

Around them, the falling snow hushed them and gave muffled groans as it was compacted beneath Hospitaller feet. From time to time, the line slowed to a stop. In the darkness ahead, Sullivan had stopped moving. In the pause of motion, Imara worried that one of them had been seen or that there was some obstruction they couldn't get around without giving themselves away. Then, Pfc Cummings would start moving again. Imara would breathe a sigh of relief and follow.

The pattern continued for a half of a kilometer, moving parallel to the valley. Soon, the treeline would bend eastward, following the slope of the hills.

Before that happened, Cpl Larson's voice crossed the comm like a voice lost down a well. "Something's coming. Behind us."

Everyone stopped.

"On our trail?" Imara asked.

"No," Larson said. A bit of good news. "They've crossed our path and are moving at an angle in the direction the patrol went. They're on a snowmobile, it's moving slow. It's small from the sounds of it. Not like the ones we saw yesterday."

Sullivan had referred to the two from Bhisho that had driven out to meet the company after the dropships had left the ground.

"Did you get a visual?"

"Did not," answered Larson. "But it did come from the

direction of the town, so that might be something."

Imara was going to ask for more information. Anything that might help her better interpret the situation. Before she could form her sentence, she heard a low octave whine deeper in the woods. The snowmobile. It wasn't passing south to north but heading deeper into the woods.

"Everyone," Imara said. "Keep the line but move west, to the right of our current direction of travel. Five meters and pause. Comm if you see or hear anything. Move now."

Imara started forward, working her way around a tree and moving toward the next one. A meter past that, she moved around another tree and then stopped. Her heads-up display showed that she had moved five meters. To her left and right, she could see the dark masses that were Pfc Cummings and Pfc Schultz. She initiated the night vision on her face shield, which allowed her to see more details. Cummings had his hand against the tree near him. Schultz was down on one knee.

When Imara looked forward, she stopped cold. The details of what she was seeing weren't entirely clear, but the hard edges indicated something specific.

"Larson, Bowers," she whispered into the comm. "Night vision. Look west. Report."

To her right, Imara could see Cummings adjusting his own shield. Likely they were all doing the same, eager to see what Imara saw. They'd be as surprised as her.

"I got armored personnel carriers," Dawson said. "At least six from here."

"I'm probably looking at another six," said Cpl Larson. "There might be more behind them."

More APCs meant more troops. If someone from the town was coming out here to meet them, and she wouldn't be surprised if it was Dmytro Barnes, they were likely to be Rhone forces. But Rhone or Serdoban, it didn't matter. Forces hiding in the woods where they were told no military units were supposed to be was a problem.

Could she get more information? Eyes would help. But if they lobbed those into the area around the APCs, they risked hitting a person or one of the vehicles. At that point, they might as well have shot up a flare or used live rounds. No, they just needed a better vantage point.

"Schultz," Imara said. To the left, she saw Schultz turn. "You grew up around trees. You ever climb them?"

Schultz came from the Jarina orphanage on Asintmah, which was known for its broad seas of forests. Tree nuts were harvested like grains from other crops. Imara knew a lot about Jarina and Asintmah because that was also where Nadia had grown up.

Imara's hand brushed against the two pocket knives nestled together at the thought of Nadia.

"I literally grew up in trees," said Schultz. "You need me to climb one?"

"I think so," said Imara. Which was all it was, just a thought. Would they collect better data with an eye strapped to a tree trunk ten or fifteen meters up?

Schultz stripped off most of her gear to climb the tree where she'd been standing. Pvt Rodriguez moved over to help Schultz reach the lower branches. The moment she grabbed the first one, it was like gravity had disappeared. Schultz was up and gone from sight in seconds. Only the occasional puff of snow, shaken from a branch, was any indication that something was moving in the tree.

Two minutes passed. Then, Schultz's voice was on the comm. "All set up, Sgt Fermo. Let me know if I need to adjust it before I come down. Nice trees, by the way."

"Good to know. Stand by, Schultz."

Imara tapped her helmet. There'd be no VR this time. She wouldn't have the sensation of floating above the ground. Instead, she had a single image with which to work. Granted, it would be at least a hundred eighty degrees horizontally and vertically, but it would still only be 2D.

When the image fluttered and then settled, Imara found herself looking out through the trees, a branch overhead shielded the eye from what little snow was still making it past the treetops. Grabbing one of the virtual controls, Imara panned down until she could see the ground. She twisted a second control with her other hand, zooming the image until she had a clear view of one of the APCs.

"Larson. Bowers," Imara said as she fine-tuned the image. "Drop in."

A few seconds later, Imara saw the icons for her two fire team leaders appear in the top right of her face shield.

"What do we have?" Bowers asked.

"Definitely APCs," said Imara. "Anyone recognize the model?"

"Allied Planets," Larson said without hesitation. "One generation out from what A.P. forces are currently using."

"Not likely to find these on the open arms market," said Imara.

Arms dealers. As long as there was war, there seemed to be someone eager to make a profit from it. The newer or more exclusive the merchandise, the greater the payout. It was one of the reasons the Hospitallers burned their electronics in the field and recycled everything when new upgrades were sent out. Hospitaller tech was the rare earth metals of the arms dealing world, difficult to find, difficult to possess, but easy to move.

"The A.P. only sells last-generation to exclusive clients and never to dealers," said Larson.

"Which means the A.P. likes someone on Abira," added Bowers.

"Maybe that someone wears a patch like the one you were given, Sarge."

"They must like them a bunch," said Imara. The count was spotty because of all the trees, but there was enough for an infantry battalion.

Imara adjusted the image, panning up several degrees and zooming in further.

"Insulated troop tents," said Bowers as the image refined itself. "They've been here a while."

"Any guesses as to where the local food supplies disappeared to?" asked Imara, though she didn't expect or need an answer. All she needed to know was that a military force three to four times larger than the Hospitaller forces at Bhisho was a serious problem.

Also a problem, continuing through the woods and risking discovery. And they couldn't go back to Grabouw even with all the information they now had. Maybe especially because of all the information they had.

"Okay, Schultz, leave the eye and come down. Everyone else, stand by." Imara adjusted the comm and pinged Maj Stewart.

The connection failed several times before she stopped trying. She'd never had a problem sending a comm request through a forest before. Perhaps it was a combination of forest, hills, and the snowstorm. She needed to get clear of the trees. But that meant going out into the snow. How safe would they be out there? Not safe at all once the storm died down. Assuming they didn't freeze to death.

Reflexively, Imara checked the power supply on her uniform. It powered the helmet computer, the comm system, and the thermal that kept her body warm enough to operate. She still had four days of normal use. Sitting in the middle of sub-freezing weather would drain it faster.

She looked east and then south. They could return to Grabouw. They could sneak into one of the other houses. They'd be safe there for a little while. That would mean going back, putting the forces hidden in the forest between her squad and the rest of the company at Bhisho.

However, there was another option. Imara had forgotten about the supposedly abandoned farmhouse on the other side of the valley until now. It was only a little further than the empty houses in Grabouw. It meant crossing the open fields, but it would put them closer to the rest of their unit. If the occupants were a family, they could apologize for the intrusion. But if it were a forward observation post for the forest hidden forces, that might be problematic.

If they had to fight, they'd draw attention. But they'd have distance in their favor, and the forest on the other side of the valley might provide a position with which to withdraw.

It wasn't the best plan. However, it was doable, and they needed to do something.

Over by the tree, Pvt Rodriguez was giving Schultz a hand getting her gear back on.

"Listen up, everyone," Imara said. She paused to make sure that Schultz and Rodriguez were paying attention before she went on.

"We're going to pull back from our current position. We're heading for the treeline. Along the way, we'll leave a couple more eyes and hands to keep watch of who's here. Then we're going to take a walk to that farmhouse they said was abandoned."

"Should be fun," Pfc Cummings said.

Imara had her doubts.

08

As they pushed through the snow on the ground and the buffeting white storm around them, Imara wondered what another squad leader would have done. Would they have risked a walk through the storm, aiming for a single building more than a kilometer away? The directionals on the HUDs worked. She'd checked them out of curiosity. But they still would have had to know the exact location of the building. Imara knew it instinctively.

Behind her, close enough so as not to lose their way, the rest of the squad followed her. More than that, they were trusting her. All but Rodriguez had experience doing just that. The trust weighed on Imara more than the snow that resisted her progress.

Trust was natural among the Hospitallers. They'd grown up trusting each other in the orphanages. They rightfully trusted their dorm mothers and fathers who so rarely let any of them down, it might as well have been never. For those that chose to enter the Orphan Corps, they went from children trusting each other to soldiers trusting each other.

As a private and private first class, Imara had never had reason to doubt the NCOs leading her. As an NCO, she'd never doubted the staff NCOs or officers. When Maj Stewart or Lt White directed her to act, she never wondered if it was the right thing to do. They'd grown up in the same places, coming up through the enlisted ranks until chosen for officer training. They were a family.

But how many family leaders took off into a snowstorm trusting their own ability to find a specific snowball amongst all that white, swirling mass? Just one that Imara could think of.

While her thoughts occupied one part of her mind, her duties occupied the other. She knew exactly where she was as she slowed to a stop. She felt the pressure of Pfc Harmon's hand against her back as she came to a complete halt.

"Check in," Imara said through the comm. When they all responded, she continued. "Twenty meters ahead."

"Never doubted you," Cpl Bowers said. Her grin was evident in her words.

"I'm still amazed," said Pvt Rodriguez.

"Let's focus." For her, the easy part was over, and now the potentially hard part was about to begin. If enemy forces were camped out in the farmhouse, things could get loud. Would it be so loud someone in Grabouw would hear it? Would some lookout in the woods hear or see it? How many of her squad would it cost? She needed to focus. Failing to do so came with a price she'd already paid once.

Imara took a breath, tapped the pocket with the two knives, and said, "Fifteen meters and Cpl Bowers goes clockwise around the house. Larson the other way. Find a door and wait. Clear?"

"Clear," the two corporals answered.

"Let's go, then." Imara started forward, the pressure of Harmon's hand on her back lessened.

The fifteen meters passed in a swirl of hissing snow. Several times, the falling snow parted, allowing Imara a brief glimpse of the farmhouse. Though it had been free of snow on the roof and windows, that was no longer the case. In fact, if it weren't for her own sense of direction and the narrow rectangles of the windows still exposed, she might have believed she'd missed the building altogether.

Imara stopped. She felt four hands tap her left shoulder and turned to watch Bowers's fireteam moving away. Four more taps and Larson's fireteam was moving right. Imara followed after Pvt Rodriguez looked back once and gave Imara a quick thumbs up that was quickly washed white in the falling snow. She gave him an easy push with one hand to remind him to keep moving.

Cpl Larson's squad pushed through the snow, occasionally leaning into the wind as it picked up speed and threw even more snow in the fireteam's way. Imara stayed close as the Hospitallers in front of her took a left turn. They stopped an arm's length from the snow wrapped farmhouse.

Imara tapped her comm so that she could talk to Larson. "That the front door?"

In response, Larson reached out and wiped away the snow. He laughed when he revealed a bare wall. He moved to his right and swiped again. His hand uncovered the door jamb and the knob.

"Nice work," Imara said. She switched over to speak to Bowers. "You find the door?"

"Yes," Bowers said. "Buried behind a meter-deep drift. It's got a window. Doesn't seem to be anyone inside."

Imara pointed at the knob, signaling Larson to try it. Simultaneously, she said to Bowers, "Try the door. Maybe we'll get lucky."

They didn't. Both doors were locked.

The comm in Imara's ear buzzed. She tapped it, adding one more person to the conversation.

"We could jimmy it." It was Pfc Walters. Imara looked at her and signaled that she should continue. "These are old-style doors. I can try it."

"You ever done it before?" Cpl Larson asked.

"Yes?"

"Been keeping secrets, Walters?" Imara teased.

"They did it on the old Saturday morning vids." Walters was extracting a long knife. The blade was wide and looked to Imara to be twenty or twenty-five centimeters in length. "I practiced on the old doors around Lalita. And then later at basic training. I might be rusty."

"Let's find out," Imara said.

Larson stepped back and waved her forward. The rest of the fireteam formed a shield around Walters. Partly they did it to block the snow, but also to watch for anyone who might use the moment to surprise them.

"Walters is trying something," Imara said into the comm.

"Thanks, Sgt Fermo. If she does get in, hurry someone across? We're getting buried in a new snowdrift."

"I got it!" Pfc Walters seemed more surprised than pleased. She backed away, sheathing her knife. The door was open several centimeters. Already the snow was blowing in through the crack.

"Cpl Larson. Let's start clearing the first floor. Bowers would like us to hurry. She says she's turning into a snowball."

Once inside, Cpl Larson's fireteam cleared the four rooms in seconds. As soon as Imara had the all clear, she stepped inside, pulling the door shut. Behind her, in the kitchen, someone was grunting while they wrestled with the door that seemed disinclined to open.

"Someone want to give me a hand?" Pfc Schultz asked. A smattering of applause caused Imara to laugh. Schultz growled and then said, "Right. Thanks, team."

Imara jogged over and lent Schultz a hand. They both pulled and got the door open several centimeters.

"Never opened a door before?" Cpl Bowers, a thick layer of snow on her helmet and shoulders, had her face pressed to the opening.

"I think the hinges are frozen. The knob certainly is."

"Push and pull," Imara said. It usually worked with rusted hinges.

With Bowers working from outside, they slammed the door shut and yanked it open. Each time around, they had the door open a little further. Pvt Rodriguez added his assistance. As they pulled the door open, he grabbed the edge of the door with Schultz and Imara. The fourth time, the door seemed to finally accept defeat. Rodriguez lost his balance, landing on his backside and sliding back half a meter.

"You okay?" Schultz asked him. She had her hand out to help him up, but he wasn't paying attention to her. "Rodriguez?"

When he did move, it was to look at Imara and signal for her to look. He pointed to a cabinet door under the counter near the broad, single pan sink. Imara followed his gaze and noticed one of the doors was slightly ajar. She held up her hand for everyone to freeze. She moved around the room and stopped next to the cabinet. On the other side, Schultz, Bowers, and Walters had their weapons pointed in Imara's direction.

Imara couldn't imagine that a Rhone soldier would choose a cabinet to hide in. But a wild animal might, if it managed to get in the building and was looking for a place to hibernate. There were a few animals on a variety of planets that, though small, were deadly if angered.

When Bowers nodded to Imara, she reached down and yanked the door of the cabinet open and then stepped back, bringing her own weapon up.

"It's a kid," Rodriguez said. He started to crawl toward the cabinet.

Imara backed away so that she had a better view. A small boy that Imara would have guessed to be five or six years of age had pulled himself as far back into the cabinet as was possible. He had a blanket wrapped around him. The boy and the blanket both looked dirty.

Rodriguez stopped short of the cabinet and sat cross-legged with both of his hands in view. "Hi," he said. "I'm Pvt Rodriguez. I'm a Hospitaller. You know what a Hospitaller is?"

The boy began to cry.

"Nice work, Rodriguez," said Pfc Harmon. She had a smirk on her face that made an easy transition to a smile.

"What? I just said hi. Can you do better?"

Harmon shook her head. "Probably not. But how about this?" She tossed Rodriguez a snow-covered T-n-T bag.

The bag exploded snow all over Rodriguez. He spluttered with the cold shock. Imara noticed that the boy stopped crying. From inside the bag, Rodriguez pulled a cloth feline and a candy stick. He leaned over and put them on the floor of the cabinet. He scooted backward so that he wasn't close enough to grab the candy and toy back. It was meant to give the child a safe space to accept the gifts if he was so inclined.

Apparently, he was. After a long pause where all the Hospitallers remained quiet and still enough that Imara could hear the snow brushing the kitchen window over the sink, the boy scooted forward and snatched the stuffed feline and candy. He scooted back as he tore the wrapper off the candy and stuck the tip into his mouth. Tears still wet his cheeks, but he seemed calmer, in Imara's opinion.

She moved near Rodriguez and knelt next to him.

"Hi. I'm Sgt Fermo. Are you afraid of Hospitallers?" The boy's eyes darted from Rodriguez to Imara and then to the other Hospitallers visible. With slow movements, he nodded yes.

"This whole world has issues," said Pfc Cummings.

"Stand down, Cummings," Imara said. She returned her attention to the boy. "I promise we won't hurt you. We actually came here to help."

The boy pulled the candy out of his mouth and then said in a voice so soft it was a good thing no one else was even breathing heavy. "They said you don't like Rhone."

"Are you Rhone?" Imara resisted the urge to move closer to better hear him.

"Yes. We all are."

Imara looked at Cpl Larson. "'We'?"

Larson turned and signaled to the other Hospitallers. They slipped out of the room and continued their search. They'd been searching for adults. Adults with weapons. Not frightened civilians.

"I promise you," Imara said as she turned back to the boy, knowing how empty the statement was. "We are here to help everyone. That's our job. That's why Pvt Rodriguez gave you the toy and the candy."

The boy clutched the toy tighter.

"You don't look comfortable," Rodriguez said. He scooted a few centimeters forward. "You want to come out and join us? We have more food."

"Food?" Imara asked in a incredulous whisper. "We have emergency rations."

"If he's hungry, he's not going to care." Rodriguez turned back to the boy. "What do you think?"

The boy had the candy back in his mouth. After a half-dozen rapid glances between Rodriguez and Imara, he scooted forward until his feet were out of the cabinet and on the ground. He stood and then slowly walked toward Rodriguez. Rodriguez held his arms out, and the boy moved far enough that Rodriguez was able to bring him into his arms. The boy moved even closer and settled on Rodriguez's lap.

"It's apple," said the boy.

"What's apple?" Rodriguez asked. He'd started a slow rocking motion with the boy held comfortably in his arms.

"The candy."

"Oh, do you like apple?"

The boy shrugged but continued to suck on the candy. Imara noticed someone had appeared at the door to the kitchen. "I'll be right back. Keep him comfortable, Rodriguez."

Imara scooted back before standing and then went into the dining room where Cpl Bowers was standing. Her eyes were on the short hallway that ended at the base of a stairwell. The stairwell turned about halfway up, disappearing around a corner.

"Find anyone else?" Imara asked.

"We think so. Sullivan found a room. It's locked. We think someone is crying on the other side."

"Okay, stand by. I'll be there in a moment."

Bowers nodded and left. Imara returned to the kitchen. Rodriguez was singing a song they'd all learned in the orphanages when they were the boy's age. A dog and a cat were best friends that liked to climb trees to see the world together. She squatted near Rodriguez but still left the boy space.

"Do you have a name?"

The boy nodded.

"What is it?" Rodriguez asked.

He was slow to pull the candy from his mouth. But when he did, he answered, "Casey."

"Casey, hi," Imara said. "You have family here?"

Casey shook his head no.

That surprised Imara. Bowers seemed confident someone else was here. "Are you alone? I mean, besides us?"

His head shook left and right. No, he wasn't alone.

09

The first thing Imara wanted to ask was, how many more? And then, who were they? Instead, she asked, "Can you tell me a name? I want to let them know you're okay."

"Cassandra," Casey said around the candy. "She's the biggest."

"Biggest? Okay, thank you, Casey."

Imara left the kitchen and went up the stairs. They doubled back on themselves, bringing Imara to the second floor. Bowers was standing at the top. She nodded and stepped aside for Imara to continue.

At the top of the stairs, there were two doors, one to each side. There were beds in both rooms, piled with blankets and quilts, and in one case, a braided rug. Two more doors revealed other rooms, stripped of blankets and bedding.

The rest of her squad was at the end of the hall. They stood against the wall on either side of the door, their weapons aimed where they were looking. Cpl Larson signaled that there was someone beyond it. Imara nodded her understanding. She went to the door and knocked softly.

"Hello?" She paused and listened. It made her skin crawl, pressing an ear to a door which she had no idea as to who was on the other side, or if they had a weapon aimed at the door. All she had to rely on was the implied age of the person, Cassandra. "If you can hear me, Casey told me that I should talk to Cassandra. Is she here?"

There was a long pause, and then, "Who are you?"

The voice was young and vibrated with fear and held-back tears.

"My name is Sgt Imara Fermo. I think you've been told bad things about us, but they aren't true. You can ask Casey. He's downstairs." Imara paused and then added, "We're Hospitallers."

There was a chorus of screams that were quickly muffled. Someone said, just loud enough for Imara to hear, "Don't let them hurt us, Cassandra."

Imara knocked on the door. The room on the other side went silent.

"Hospitallers don't hurt," Imara said. "It's our duty to provide aid and protection to those who need it. Casey trusts us. He's downstairs with one of my people. Do you want to talk to him?"

"Yes!" It was Cassandra's voice again.

Imara turned and signaled to Cpl Bowers. Bowers disappeared and returned a minute later with Rodriguez, who was carrying Casey. Imara waved for them to continue down the hall.

"Casey's here," Imara said to the door. She turned and spoke to Casey. "Can you tell Cassandra that it's okay to come out?"

When he nodded in the affirmative, Rodriguez stepped closer to the door, turning so that Casey was closest.

"Cassandra," he said. "They got candy!"

Behind her, Imara caught the quieted giggles of several of her people. She shook her head in mock disbelief.

Cassandra spoke. Her voice sounding as though she had moved closer to the door. "Are you okay, Casey? Did they hurt you?"

"No. They gave me a kitty and candy. It tastes like apple."

Imara turned to the rest of the Hospitallers. "I hope you all got stuff in your bags."

Her words cause a rush of bag checks among her squad. Several of them held up small toys and candies wrapped in brightly colored cellophane. She gave them a thumbs up just as the lock on the door clicked.

The door opened slowly, swinging inward. A girl, her face streaked in several places with ash, her hair matted and uncombed, held the door as it opened. Behind her, Imara saw a bathtub where four other children huddled together, holding each other and a wildly colored quilt.

No one in the hall moved. Even though none of them were Shepherds, they'd all received some basic training on working with orphans in extreme situations. They'd all been orphans themselves. As eager as they were, Imara knew they didn't want to exacerbate the situation by rushing forward.

"See? Apple!" Casey proudly held the candy out for Cassandra to see.

"Neat, Casey." Cassandra turned to Imara, seeming to recognize her as the one who had spoken through the door. "Do you have food? We haven't eaten in a couple days."

"We have emergency rations," Imara said. She wasn't quite willing to call them food, raising the expectations of the children only to have those expectations dashed at the first dry, difficult to chew bite. As much as Hospitallers groaned at having to eat them, they knew the rations would keep them alive. At times, that was all that mattered. Perhaps the children behind Cassandra felt the same. "Can we go downstairs? There's a bit more room."

When Cassandra nodded agreement, Imara sent the other Hospitallers ahead. She and Pvt Rodriguez, who still carried Casey, walked with Cassandra to the stairs. The other four children trailed behind, eager yet cautious.

In the main sitting room of the farmhouse, the Hospitallers had pushed the furniture to the walls, opening the space in the middle. Most of them sat on the floor. Pfc Harmon was watching out a front window. Pfc Walters was in the kitchen doing the same through another window. Those on the floor had pulled out emergency rations, candy, and enough small toys that the children could have their pick.

One of the trailing children, on seeing the candy, looked around and then said, "I don't like apple."

Cassandra put her hand on the little girl's shoulder. "This is Lucy. She doesn't like whatever it is the other kids are having."

Pfc Sullivan held up four candies. "None of these are apple. Which one would you like?"

"Not apple," Lucy said.

Sullivan picked one of the candies and held it out. "This one is strawberry."

"I like strawberry." Lucy stepped forward and took the candy. She fumbled with the wrapper and, after several tries, held it out to Pfc Sullivan. "Please, may you open it?"

Smiling, Sullivan took the candy and quickly shucked the

wrapper and handed it back. It disappeared just as fast into Lucy's mouth.

"Who else do we have here?" Imara asked.

Cassandra went to a boy who looked a little older than Casey. "This is Billy."

"I wasn't scared," Billy said. He had his hands rolled up in the hem of his shirt, one finger worrying at a small hole.

"Because you're brave," Imara said. She nodded to Cassandra, who moved over to two girls. Except for their clothes, they looked exactly alike.

Cassandra was like a magnet for the girls. They moved in close to the older girl, clutching at her shirt sleeves. "Jodi and Vanessa," said Cassandra. "They're sisters."

"Twins," said Cpl Bowers. "I had two brothers in my first squad. They fought all the time."

"We don't fight," one of the girls said. Imara already didn't know which one was which. It got worse when they both said at the same time, "Can we have candy, too?"

Pfc Sullivan walked on his knees over to where Cassandra now served as a shield for the two girls. He held both hands out with several candies in each. Like striking vipers, the twins' hands shot out and snatched a candy each.

"Cassandra?" Sullivan asked, holding his hand higher for her.

She took one without looking and pushed it into a pocket of her pants. "You said there was food?"

"Rations, yes," Imara said. "But maybe you could tell me where your parents are?"

"Dead," Cassandra said. Her eyes were emotionless as she said it. As if she'd had to explain it so many times, it no longer carried the weight it should.

"I'm sorry." And she was. Many Hospitallers didn't talk about it, but Imara knew that many of them, who'd been orphaned very young, wished they could have at least remembered their family. "Is this where they died?"

And if it was, why were the children still here?

"No," said Cassandra. "We're not from here. We were brought to the town by Rhone soldiers. They said the people of the town would take care of us because we're Rhone, too. But they didn't. They told us we had to leave. We tried to walk to where the Serdobans live, but it snowed. We came here. I climbed through a window and let everyone in. The heat went out a few days ago. It's been cold."

"I believe it has been," Imara said. "Very cold."

"And we didn't have any food," Jodi, one of the twins said.

"Well, you can have food now. Such as it is." Imara stood. "Bowers, can you handle this. I need to see if I can open a line to Maj Stewart."

"Will do, Sergeant." Bowers rubbed her hands together. "Okay, who's ready for an eating adventure?"

Imara left Bowers to her machinations and went back upstairs. The rooms at the top of the stairs were on the side of the house that pointed toward Bhisho. From the front of the house to the back, the difference in distance to Bhisho was negligible. But there were fewer walls to interfere.

She tapped the comm for the connection. Just as quickly, she brought the volume down. The burst of static hurt physically. She sent the request three times before the connection took on the other side.

The major's voice was thin, like talking through a wall. "Sgt Fermo? Everything okay?"

"Not sure, Major. A lot of things have been happening."

There was a pause before the major spoke again. "What's happening? I'm sorry, Fermo, the storm is messing with the comm."

Imara overrode the controls on her comm system and began making small adjustments to the frequency. She managed to remove some of the static.

"We left Grabouw, Major."

"Where are you?"

Another small adjustment to the comm cleaned up the major's voice. She hoped it was doing the same on his end. Or that he was doing the same.

"We're in a farmhouse near the pass." The major seemed to hear her well enough for the moment. She continued with her update, explaining why they left and how they made the discovery of the hidden troops.

"Have to be Rhone," the major said. "Unless the Serdobans were planning an attack on Grabouw. That seems unlikely. The Serdobans want peace between the factions more than the Rhone do. The question is, what are they doing there?"

"Supplies?" Imara suggested. She shared her concern that it was this military that stole all the food from the Bhisho warehouses and had pretty much done the same thing in Grabouw but with less violence. She ended with, "I think most of the supplies we brought here are going to end up in the hands of the soldiers."

"Not to sound picky, Sgt Fermo, but where are my crawlers?"

Imara laughed and didn't hide it. "Disabled, Major. They won't move until Cpl Larson enters whatever passcode she's put in them."

"Good thinking. Do you have enough supplies?"

"Maybe," said Imara. She recounted the discovery of the children. Then, "I thought we'd leave at first light at the earliest, sunset at the latest."

"Might be longer than that," Maj Stewart said. "The storm blowing through seems to be gathering strength. As long as you're safe, you should just stay put. Skies clear up long enough, the rest of the battalion will drop down and then we'll come and get you."

The image of a battalion of APCs rolling across the snow-covered fields in the morning light was a satisfying thought to Imara. "We'll be looking forward to it, Major."

"All right. Let me hear back from you in six. And get some rest."

"Will do." Imara cut the comm. She'd sat down at some moment in the conversation and hadn't really been paying attention to it. Now that she did, though, she realized they'd been moving for close to twenty hours non-stop.

If she was tired, everyone else must be tired. She pushed herself up from the bed and went back down to the living area. She was surprised by the quiet until she had a good look at what had happened. Each of the children had fallen asleep, Cassandra included. She was sleeping on a couch, curled into a fetal position.

The other children, though, were like Casey, secure in a Hospitaller's arms, their own dangling by their sides as they slept the sleep of someone who was safe and loved.

Imara had slept like that when she was young. The memories were faint, but she could recall several times having a hard time sleeping and her dorm mother holding her through half the night.

"What'd the major say?" asked Cpl Bowers.

"Storm," Imara said. "We're stuck here for a while. He said we should rest."

"Good idea, Sarge. You first."

Imara shook her head. "Not yet. You and Larson now. I'll wake one of you in two. We'll rotate with one of the others for a second lookout."

"Can't talk you out of it?" Bowers asked.

Imara knew Bowers knew better but understood that she had to at least try.

"Those are my orders," said Imara.

10

Imara didn't typically dream of coffee. She dreamed of battles, stained-glass memories of her childhood at the orphanage, holding hands with Nadia when no one was around. But coffee? No. Which meant something else.

She wasn't dreaming.

Imara opened her eyes and looked around, sniffing the air. The coffee was real, and she was alone. She sat up, pushing against one of the two couches and tilted her head. Yes, there were sounds. Murmured conversation in the direction of the kitchen. But also, laughter, from upstairs. She stood and stretched out the sore muscles from sleeping on the floor. It was something she'd never gotten used to and doubted she ever would.

A quick glance at the windows showed nothing but snow. But it was bright, which meant it was day. Maybe the storm had worn itself out. If that were the case, they could be on their way. Or, at the least, help was on their way.

She grabbed her helmet and secured it before walking into the kitchen.

"Morning," she said.

"Morning, Sgt Fermo," Cpl Larson said. He was leaning against a counter. Sitting on the counter next to him was Billy. He was happily chewing on something that wasn't a piece of apple candy.

"Is that a pancake?" And now that she'd asked it, she realized there'd been more than coffee in the air. "And coffee, too? How?"

Larson pointed down. "We went to the basement to change the house batteries. The kids didn't know they were down there."

"Didn't help that the door was bolted shut," said Pfc Schultz. She was sitting at the table with Lucy on her lap. A comb was in her hand, and Lucy's hair looked shiny and smooth.

"We took care of the door," Larson said. "When we were down there, dealing with the batteries, Walters found the storeroom."

"Whoever lived here left in as much a hurry as those from the house we were sent to," said Pfc Walters. "But this house was farther away from the others and locked tight."

"And they had coffee?" Imara said.

Cpl Larson nodded. "Yes. Ground and in a can, but still coffee."

"We'll have to leave contact information," Imara said. Hospitallers didn't normally pillage the places they visited. Having the need for shelter and then finding orphans in need of food had required that they act. Unlike other military forces, the Hospitallers would compensate the owners, and usually at a higher rate than the going market value.

"Already did," Walters said. She brought Imara a cup of coffee. "The syrup is synthetic, but it's still good quality. And rehydrated potatoes that fried up really well."

Imara took the coffee and sipped it. It was definitely can-stored and had been so for a long while. Even still, it was a bit better than Insta. A hundred times better than nothing at all.

Cpl Larson had grabbed a plate while Imara sampled the coffee. "Pancakes, Sergeant?"

"In a minute. Where's Cpl Bowers's team?"

Pfc Schultz laughed and then said, "Upstairs. The bathroom."

"All right. I'll be back in a minute." Imara took her coffee cup with her and went down the hall toward the stairs. Along the way, she discovered the door to the basement. Her people hadn't broken the lock or kicked in the door. Instead, they'd pulled the trim and removed the entire door jamb, setting everything to one side.

As she climbed the stairs, the laughter grew in volume. It seemed to rise with the sound of splashing water. She followed the noises along the upstairs hall to the bathroom.

Inside the bathroom, Cpl Bowers was kneeling at the edge of the tub, her sleeves rolled up. The twins, Vanessa and Jodi, were in the tub, the water slightly brown. Bowers had piled soap bubbles on their heads. They were now trying to blow the soap off each other's heads. Cassandra, who seemed to have already had a bath, was now wrapped in a towel. She stood by the toilet, her back to Pfc Harmon. Harmon had a comb and was running it through Cassandra's hair.

"Having fun?"

Cpl Bowers looked over as Imara spoke. "Hey, Sgt Fermo. With the back-up batteries online, we thought the kids could all use a bath."

"They seem to be enjoying it." Imara turned to Cassandra. "How are you doing? How are the other kids doing?"

"We're okay, I guess. Thank you for turning on the power and finding the food."

"Thank you, but I think you'll have to thank those who actually did the real work," said Imara. "I'll be back."

Back in the hallway, Imara went to one of the rooms where the beds had been piled with blankets and quilts. She was now well aware as to why the bedding had been piled. In the room nearest the stairs, she found Pvt Rodriguez and the little boy, Casey. Several boxes of clothes were on the floor. One looked like it had vomited its content of clothing over the floor near and around Rodriguez and Casey.

"This room will never pass inspection," Imara said. She leaned against the door jamb and sipped from her cup of quickly cooling coffee. She'd have to return to the kitchen for a warmer, PDQ.

"Morning, Sgt Fermo," Pvt Rodriguez said. He was kneeling on the ground, holding a small pair of pants by the waist. Casey, with his hands on Rodriguez's shoulders, was attempting to step into the legs of the pants.

Casey looked over at Imara, missing the pant leg he'd been aiming for. "They found clothes. Clean clothes."

"Where did we find clothes?"

"In the basement," Rodriguez said. He shifted the pants he was holding so that Casey's next attempt brought his foot cleanly into the leg opening. "Whoever lived here was thrifty. They saved clothes and bedding in air-tight containers. They were even marked."

Rodriguez used his chin to point Imara's attention to the boxes.

The one that had spewed its contents had the word 'boys' and then '5-8' written in precise lettering on one side. The box next to that had 'girls' with the same age range. Too small for Cassandra, but maybe they'd already solved that problem. And what about winter clothes?

"Good work. But, let's make sure that we leave this house in good condition before we part."

"We leaving soon?" asked Pvt Rodriguez. He was tugging the pants over Casey's hips, lifting the boy several times, which caused the boy to giggle.

"Hopefully."

Imara left and returned to the kitchen. Everyone nodded to her as she entered. Once there, she belatedly realized that Billy and Lucy were clean and wearing fresh clothes. She helped herself to a half-cup of coffee. At the same time, Cpl Larson made another pancake for Billy, who seemed capable of eating every pancake ever made. Lucy and Pfc Harmon had switched places. Harmon's helmet was on the table, and Lucy was pulling the comb through the Hospitaller's short hair.

"Reminds me of home," Imara said. Home being the orphanage. Sometimes the older kids would come down and entertain the younger ones. On Saturday mornings, the dorm parents would usually cook breakfast rather than going to the cafeteria so the kids could eat and watch morning vids. There was nothing quite as comfortable as eating fresh pancakes while watching Heroes of the Galaxy making everything right that had been wrong. Then they'd play in the yards if it was nice out, indoors if not, and the dorm parents were always there.

"Except for the snow," Pfc Harmon said. "We rarely had snow. Unless we took a field trip up to the mountains. Still, never this much snow."

Which reminded Imara. "We should probably check on the weather. Maybe we'll get lucky and can head out, meet the rest of the company halfway."

The comb clattered to the ground.

"You're leaving us?" Lucy's eyes were beginning to back up with tears. Harmon quickly wrapped her in a hug.

"We've no plans on leaving you," Imara said. She just assumed, and likely so had the rest of the company, that the children would come with them. Maj Stewart would call in a Shepherd who would track down family or make other arrangements for the children. If they had no family at all, they could be transferred to another planet. There wasn't an orphanage on Abira.

"You'll come with us," said Cpl Larson. He set a platter of pancakes on the table. Billy had one in each hand, both of them missing sizable chunks.

"We'll keep you safe," Pfc Harmon said. She squeezed Lucy into a hug until the girl giggled for help.

"And if you want to check the weather, Sarge," Larson said, "you're going to have to dig your way out."

To prove his point, he opened the back door, which took a little extra effort, to reveal a wall of snow bearing an impression of the door.

"Second floor?"

"Maybe," Larson said as he leaned against the door to compel it to close. "You want me to go look?"

"No, that's okay, Larson. My idea."

Once more, Imara took the stairs, this time without a coffee cup. She turned left at the top and entered the room she'd sat in while talking to the C.O. There was one window. Pulling back the curtain showed a swirling world of white. The snow was piled up to just below the window ledge but sloped downward for several meters. She left and crossed the hall.

The snow here wasn't as deep, being on the leeward side of the storm. Still, the snow was up over the windows. The storm was the real concern. They could dig out of the snow, but if the storm was going to keep dumping on them, it might be better to wait.

Overhead, the clouds hung dense but bright. The lighting was flat. Imara could see the tops of several of the taller buildings in Grabouw. Leaning to the right and peering left, she could see the dark, jagged lines of the trees on the other side of the valley. The opposite way, the trees were just as covered in snow, but physically closer. Maybe if they made for the woods.

She'd have to check in with Maj Stewart and get his opinion.

Now was as good a time as any. She tapped the comm but was interrupted by a beeping alarm. She pulled down her face shield. Top left, in red, were the words, motion detected.

Imara stepped into the hallway and bellowed, "Did anyone leave hands anyplace besides the woods?"

Cpl Bowers appeared at the bathroom door, Cassandra holding her hand. Rodriguez stepped out of the bedroom. Boots on the stairs tugged at her attention. She turned to see Cpl Larson taking them two at a time.

"An alarm go off?" Larson asked.

"Yes." Imara looked at the others. "The woods? That's the only place we've left hands?"

"Yes, Sergeant," Bowers said. Rodriguez nodded in agreement.

"Agreed," Larson said. "No one in my fireteam has dropped a hand or eye since we left the woods."

"Okay, thank you. Carry on." Imara returned to the bedroom and tapped the system to access the hands and eyes they'd left behind.

The hands closest to where they'd found the military encampment were all registering vibrations. The simple catalog in the system suggested it was tracked-vehicle movement, but not a lot. Imara switched to the eyes. She started with the two left at the forest edge. They'd been attached to the inner side of the tree trunks to avoid being buried in snow. One of them, though, was useless as a snow-laden branch had bent far enough to cover the cameras. The other showed nothing more than tree trunks and snow.

She switched to the next two eyes and found a similar situation. Nothing was showing except for trees. So, she switched over to the first eye they'd placed. It was still working, though she'd wondered if she'd gone back to one of the other eyes by accident. A quick scan left and then right revealed she was in the right place. The tents were still in place.

It was the APCs that were missing.

11

Imara quickly moved through the other cameras. They were all facing inward.

"Larson!"

She scanned with several other eyes, seeing nothing. The hands still registered movement.

Boots boomed as they bounded up the stairs.

"Sgt Fermo?"

"Drop in here with me. I can't find the APCs."

"The ones in the woods?"

Imara paused. Was that movement? She widened the view of the eye she was looking through and laughed.

"Sergeant?"

"Come look." A green icon appeared in the top right of the face shield. Larson was in. "I thought I saw someone moving. See it?"

Larson laughed after a second. "Looks a lot like a squirrel."

"I'd bet it's the Abira equivalent. Now, where'd the vehicles go?"

"May I have the controls?"

"Yes." Imara tapped several virtual controls. They turned red, signaling that she was no longer in charge of them. "Yours."

The image started to flash as Cpl Larson ran through all the eyes to verify Imara's conclusion. At one point, he scanned and jumped to a different eye quickly enough that Imara almost fell off the bed she'd been sitting on.

Then the colors changed. Cpl Larson was cycling through IR and thermal. Imara had done the same thing, but Larson had a finesse when it came to VR and the eyes.

"Here," he said. "Near this tree."

A pointer appeared on Imara's image of the forest in thermal. A harsh red spot still glowed on one of the trees.

"Either a vehicle was running its heater while too close to the tree, or someone peed."

"That high?" Imara asked.

"Good point."

Imara dropped out of visual and slapped her helmet face-shield up. "Keep looking. I'm going to get us another view."

She left Cpl Larson to pull as much information as he could. There was a possibility that she was being paranoid, but there was only one way she could think of to determine if that was all it was. She started down the stairs, shouting for Pfc Cummings to join her.

"Hey, Sgt Fermo," Cummings said. He'd moved fast enough that he was only one step behind Imara as she reached the bottom landing.

"You have any eyes?" Imara was already walking toward the front door. In the kitchen, she heard one of the children laughing.

"Got three," Cummings said. He tapped the pouch where they were stored. "What do you want to do?"

Imara pulled the front door open, revealing a short wall of snow. "I want to launch at least one. And as high as it can go."

Snow collapsed off the wall and cascaded into the house. More snow swirled in the air. The sky might not be clear, but machines generated heat, and that was all that mattered. Imara pushed into the snow, lifting her feet high and stepping forward. She used her hands, shoving the snow to the side, creating a tunnel as she moved more of the snow out of the way.

Behind her, the door clicked shut. Hopefully, it was unlocked. Other sounds followed her as Cummings switched out the barrels on his weapon. Hospitaller multi-use weapons had a variety of switchable barrels, stocks, and receivers. The trigger and firing mechanism were the heart of the MUW around which everything else was customizable.

"Here should be enough," Imara said. She kicked and swiped at the snow. Then the ceiling overhead collapsed, temporarily covering her and Cummings. She shook it off before kicking and pushing to create a small clearing. She then turned to face the direction of the pass.

"Straight up?" Cummings asked. He was slipping a charge into the receiver. As he dropped an eye down the barrel, he added, "Or an angle?"

Straight up would give the greatest height, but an angle might provide them a better chance at discovering the location of the APCs if this was where they were heading. "Angle, Cummings. But not much. We wouldn't want the eye to hit someone on the head and give our presence away."

"Good idea," Cummings said. He stowed the standard barrel that he'd been holding under one arm while connecting the grenade launcher that would put the eye into the air. He looked over to Imara while she was sliding her face shield into place, tapping the side of her helmet as she did. "You're not going to ride up, are you, Sergeant?"

"With my eyes closed." Imara had made the mistake of observing through an eye from the moment it was launched. She'd been a private and had never used the newest iteration of eye technology. It was like riding the fastest rollercoaster with nothing to hold onto. She'd thrown up before she'd even realized she was sick to her stomach.

There were good reasons why someone would want to observe en route besides the thrill. Data would be collected and could be analyzed at leisure. Imara knew they didn't have the time to spare, not if the APCs were rolling toward Bhisho.

"You setting a max altitude alert?" Cummings had loaded the eye and was making adjustments to his heads-up display. It would let him know when he had the optimum angle of fire and when to pull the trigger.

Imara's VR was all black. She bent her knees and worked at centering herself, so she maintained her balance. "Near max," she said. "I want to start scanning the moment the eye is at maximum. Whenever you're ready, Cummings."

The snow crunched as Pfc Cummings adjusted his stance. Cold wafted up under Imara's shield, cooling her cheeks.

"Firing," Cummings muttered. His single word was followed by the whomp-noise of the propellant exploding in the barrel, shoving the eye skyward. "Good launch, Sgt Fermo."

Imara offered a thumb's up that she couldn't see. Her focus was on the rapidly increasing numbers on the edge of her VR. They were red at first, slowly transitioning to orange, then yellow. She closed her eyes just at a soft bell chimed in her ears. Then she opened her eyes and tried not to fall over.

All around her, Imara saw snow and clouds and an absence of ground. It never failed to impress. Occasionally it knocked her over. This time she maintained her balance and quickly panned down to look for the surface of Abira.

After a brief pause, the eye began to fall groundward. Snow hurtled past. In places, the amount of falling snow would lessen, allowing for brief glimpses of the ground. Several times she thought she saw large black dots on the landscape, but they were quickly hidden by more swirls of snow. Just as she was beginning to doubt that the APCs had started toward Bhisho, there was an extended break in the snow.

"There they are," Imara said. She reached out and tapped virtual controls to record still images. "Not just APCs."

The snow collapsed the break Imara had been watching through. She staggered back and tapped her helmet to close the connection. Her view was immediately flooded with bright white snow and the gray column that was Pfc Cummings.

"You saw more than APCs?"

Imara shoved her face shield up. She took a moment to orient herself and then started kicking her way through the snow and back to the house. "Yeah, IFVs and cannons."

All the APCs Imara had seen when they were in the woods had the usual machine guns mounted on top. But there hadn't been any sign of autocannons or artillery. Now there was. And there were a lot more vehicles than she'd initially estimated.

"Come on, Cummings, get inside before we lose you in the snow."

The door opened with a turn of the knob. Imara tramped in, knocking snow off her uniform and equipment with each heavy stomp. The stomping noise she made was loudly echoed as

Cummings entered the room and began knocking the snow off of himself in the same manner.

Several Hospitallers hurried into the living room. Imara noticed them, but she was also moving past them, heading for the stairs.

"What happened?" asked Cpl Bowers.

"Ask Cummings," Imara said as she rounded the first flight.

"I don't know what happened!" Cummings called after Imara.

Imara was already tapping her comm plate. "Then you'll have to wait."

She turned into the first room as she'd done the night before. The comm request was responded to quicker than the night before.

"Sgt Fermo." It was Maj Stewart. "How was the night?"

"Quiet, Major. But the morning has just gotten more interesting."

Imara explained about seeing the APCs and infantry fighting vehicles with their auto-cannons and heavy machine guns. She emphasized the numbers.

"That's a bit more than half a regiment," the major said. His words were softened with musing. "Or they're spread thin. Either way, we are very likely outnumbered."

"Maybe there's something we can do here?" asked Imara. They were only one squad, but they could cause quite a distraction if it was needed. They might pay a high price for it, but what would the rest of the company be paying if they didn't.

The major didn't hear Imara's laugh, but his own sounded like a response to what had been going through her head. Instead of a direct response to her thoughts, Maj Stewart said, "Well, if you had a landing beacon in your pocket, Fermo."

"Why a landing beacon, Major?" She didn't have one. They were only deployed in extreme circumstances that made visual and computer landings difficult.

"Because ours appears to have accidentally been broken," said the major. "And then there's this snowstorm. It's let up a bit down here, but above, in the clouds, it appears to be playing havoc with the nav systems. A lot of ions or something clever that was described to me a few hours ago. The point, Sergeant, is that nothing is coming down until the weather eases or another landing beacon falls out of an unmarked box."

"Do we know when the weather will back off?" Imara asked. Maybe it was possible to keep the opposing forces at bay that long.

"Forty-eight hours." Major Stewart didn't sound pleased. "And because of the ceasefire, we didn't come laden with enough ammo for a sustained battle."

"We should at least attempt to rejoin the rest of the company," said Imara. She was feeling helpless. It was a feeling she didn't like. Even less so since Nadia's death. She wanted to have some sort of control over her situation, even if it meant kicking a hornets' nest.

"No, Sgt Fermo. Even if you went around, it'd take too long, and you'd likely be discovered. I can't spare another squad for a rescue. Lay low and wait until the weather clears. Then contact us. If we don't respond, contact the ship."

Imara wanted to argue but knew that would solve nothing. Sometimes the odds were against them. This seemed to be one of those times. "Yes, Major."

"Never forgotten, Sgt Fermo."

"Always remembered, Maj Stewart."

The comm connection clicked. Maj Stewart had ended the conversation by closing the line. Imara absentmindedly tapped her own comm as she sat on the bare mattress. This was how it felt when the information had come over the comm. Cpl Nadia Weddle and her fireteam caught in a crossfire. The rest of the platoon had responded with prejudice, wiping out most of the company that had killed Nadia and her people.

Several more lives had almost been lost in Imara's squad as the news came across and she'd been unable to act for several minutes. It took the platoon staff sergeant bellowing across the comm to snap her back to the present and her duties.

This time she was ready. This time she wasn't incapable of acting. She just wasn't being allowed to act.

Imara swallowed her pride with a gulp of frustration and returned to the ground floor. The rest of her squad had come down either while she'd been outside with Cummings or while she was on the comm with Maj Stewart.

"Cummings says he doesn't know anything," Cpl Larson said. He grinned at the end. It pulled a reluctant smile from Imara.

"That's never stopped him before," she said.

"Hey." Pfc Cummings' petulance was artificial, which made it all the funnier to the rest of the squad. The children smiled with their mouths. Their eyes flashed confusion.

"You're back," Cpl Bowers said. "So, now you can tell us what's going on."

Imara nodded. "I can. The unit we saw in the woods last night? They're on the move, heading toward Bhisho. Normally wouldn't be a problem, but the storm is making resupply and reinforcements impossible. Forty-eight hours before things are clear enough for dropships to come down."

"We've dropped in bad weather plenty of times," said Pfc Harmon. She was holding the little girl, Lilly, who was holding a farmer doll.

"But not weather like this," Imara said. "It's the type of weather and the conditions."

"Landing beacon." Pfc Walters brought one hand down to the other, letting the fingers interlace.

"Except, the landing beacon that came with us seems to have had an accident."

"Shouldn't need one," said Cpl Larson. Then, "But the storm, yeah, that's going to be trouble."

"What if we had one?" asked Pfc Walters.

"We don't," Pfc Sullivan said.

"But what if we did." Walters was persistent. Imara also noticed a gleam in her eyes.

"If we did," Imara said. "Then they'd land a bunch of dropships and make whoever it is in the APCs regret the idea of attacking."

"But since we don't have one, what do we do?" asked Cpl Bowers.

Walters was grinning. There was no mistaking the only kid with the answer in the classroom. "I don't know," Imara said. "What do we do, Pfc Walters?"

"Build one."

12

Everyone looked at Walters like she was a little bit crazy. The grin on her face didn't help her position.

"I don't know about anyone else," Pvt Rodriguez said. "But I didn't bring any spare landing beacon parts with me. Anyone else?"

Sullivan, Cummings, and Schultz all patted their pockets and shook their heads and then laughed.

"We might not have parts," said Cpl Larson. "However, if Walters is suggesting we build a landing beacon, she must have an idea. You see something in the house, Walters?"

"Not this house." She pointed south. "Back in Grabouw. The one with all the antennas and the dish? You don't have that much on the roof without something interesting inside."

"Listening post," Bowers said. She was nodding her understanding of Walters's implication. "If it's still active, they'd not only have everything we'd need, they'd have the power to run it, too."

"We're just going to walk up and knock on the door? 'Excuse me, Sir or Madam, do you have any spare parts we can borrow to build a landing beacon to vanquish your allies?'"

"Sullivan," Imara said, addressing his comment. "I don't think we're going to ask. Those are Rhone. Likely the military on the valley floor is Rhone. And there's at least one person in the town who isn't local."

"What was his name?" Walters asked more to herself than to anyone else. Then, "Ah! Dmytro. Mr. Dmytro Barnes."

One of the twins had wandered over to Imara and tugged at her hand. Imara picked the girl up. "How are you feeling today, Vanessa?"

"I'm Jodi!"

"Of course you are." And that reminded Imara. "We can't take the kids with us. Are we taking volunteers to remain behind?"

No one stepped forward. It was what Imara expected from her people. There was action to be had. None of them wanted to remain behind while there was.

"If you're coming back, it's okay." Everyone turned and looked at Cassandra. She had the other twin in tow. "Are you coming back?"

"Yes," said Imara. "But we'll have to leave again to set out the beacon."

Cpl Bowers reached out and put a hand on Cassandra's shoulder. "But we'd be coming back again, too. And that's when we'll take you all someplace safe."

"We've done okay for weeks out here," Cassandra said. Imara couldn't miss the sadness behind the flat tones of Cassandra's words. "Now we have power and food. We can look after ourselves."

Some of the children looked unsure. Doubtless, they feared being abandoned again.

"We will return," Imara said. "We don't leave anyone behind."

Cassandra nodded. A whisper of a smile touched her lips. Imara was not going to let her down.

"When do we go?" Cpl Larson asked. His question brought everyone's attention back to the freshly minted mission. "And do we travel light?"

"We need to go soon," Imara said. "It's daylight, but it's also snowing heavily now. We might as well be invisible. You can leave packs, and non-combat essentials staged here. We'll leave in thirty."

Jodi tapped the side of Imara's face. "Can we have more pancakes?"

The snow kept coming. Imara wondered if there was any liquid water left on Abira. Did the whole world turn into a snowball during the cyclic deep winter? A winter so long and cold, they broke it into two seasons to reflect the frigid weather that brought them to midwinter with still two and a half months of wintertide to go.

If they died out here, how long until someone found their bodies?

"By your leave, Sgt Fermo."

Imara had been pushing through the deep-piled snow, creating a narrow canyon that the others followed. They minimized their disturbance in the hopes that if someone in the town just happened to look their way just as the falling snow slacked off, they wouldn't see a squad of Hospitallers bounding along, intent on raiding their home.

Pushing through the snow was hard work, and they'd been taking turns every ten minutes. Imara had gone last. Before that, she'd remained just behind the person on point to correct their direction of travel as necessary. All of the signals from the ship, the company back at Bhisho, and the satellites that would have been useful for navigation were all in disarray. Someone had suggested there might have been either high metal ion count in the snow or in the atmosphere, which was exacerbated by the cold and wind.

It didn't matter to Imara. Others would have aimed and likely missed, wasting valuable time, but she had not only directed them unerringly to the town, she'd bring them to the doorstep of the very house that was their destination.

So, she pushed into the wall of snow to her right and let Pvt Rodriguez take point. "All yours, Rodriguez."

He stepped past her and began kicking and shoving through the snow, tearing out a ragged pass for all of them.

"To the right, Rodriguez. Just a little."

He laughed and adjusted his forward motion. "I just started, Sergeant."

"You started wrong."

Rodriguez drove forward for ten minutes, quickly replaced by Pfc Sullivan. While the squad pushed on, Rodriguez would get a small break to catch his breath and drink a couple sips of water. Imara hadn't stopped for a breather. She'd kept going. Someone had to drive the train.

Her second time at the front, Imara paused.

"Everything okay, Sgt Fermo?" asked Rodriguez. He spoke in a hush as they were now in the town, the peaks of several roofs barely visible.

They'd passed several well-cut pathways through the snow. They aligned with the town's streets and would have been useful for cutting down their own travel time, but that would have increased their chances of being discovered. So, Imara had them continue to blaze their own trail, hoping that anyone who saw it would be too cold to bother investigating.

And that had brought them to the house with the antennas.

"We're here," Imara said.

"I don't see anything," Cpl Bowers said from behind Rodriguez.

In response, Imara pushed away some of the snow at face level. A door window was revealed as the snow was brushed away.

"I'm still amazed," Bowers said. "We going to knock?"

"No. Get Walters up here."

A few moments of whispers brought Pfc Walters to where Imara was standing. She traded places with Rodriguez to get closer to the door.

"Well?" Imara asked.

Walters brushed away the snow around the doorknob and lock. She looked at it for several seconds and then shook her head.

"It's not as old as the one at the farm," she said. "But the wood is in bad shape. We could probably carve out the strike plate in the doorway frame."

"You want to do it?"

"Cummings would be better at it, Sgt Fermo. He's stronger."

Cummings was called for. Rodriguez and Walters moved back to give him room when he arrived.

"Walters wants you to dig out the strike plate in the door frame," Imara said.

"Quietly?"

Imara smiled and shook her head. "Yes, quietly. Otherwise, we might as well knock."

"On it." Cummings pulled out a fixed-blade knife, knelt in the snow, and began digging at the wood.

Immediately, Imara could see that it was wet and partially rotted. Either people didn't care, or they weren't concerned. Or, just maybe, everyone in Grabouw knew what the house was and wasn't foolish enough to enter.

Imara tapped her comm and whispered, "Cpl Larson, make sure we have someone watching our backside."

"Will do, Sergeant," Larson whispered back.

They'd been proceeding in ten-minute increments all the way from the farm. And though it took Cummings a little less than ten minutes, it felt twice as long before he held up a shiny, metallic plate still gripping wood with its screws.

"Okay, everyone in position. Bowers, your team on point. Let's clear the space as quickly as we can, but be thorough. If we can avoid a firefight, that would be preferable."

"And check the cupboards, too," Pfc Harmon whispered. No one laughed in appreciation, but they did grin and nod agreement.

"Okay, team," Bowers said, her voice all business. "Harmon, Sullivan got left. Cummings. You're with me. Stand back, Sgt Fermo."

Imara brought her rifle up, pressing the butt of the stock into the space where her shoulder and arm met. As Harmon and Cummings flanked the door, Imara took her weapon off safe mode. She had a gut feeling they wouldn't face any resistance, but that didn't mean they shouldn't plan for the off chance that she was wrong.

"Now," whispered Bowers.

Harmon put her hand to the door and pushed. It swung open slowly. The barrel of Cummings' weapon entered the space, tracking left. He pulled back as the door opened further. Harmon brought her weapon up and tracked right. As they both kept watch on either side of the room, Bowers and Sullivan slipped in.

Several seconds later, Harmon and Cummings slipped into the room. Imara could see from her position that it was a large entryway. This wasn't a simple home. It was more of a manor. Being near the center of town and standing alone, it had likely been or still was the home of a prosperous farmer or merchant.

A merchant with a lot of tech somewhere.

The pairs entered doorways to the left and right.

"Pardon us, Sgt Fermo." Cpl Larson had put his hand on Imara's shoulder as he spoke in a hushed voice.

Imara nodded and moved to the left. Larson's fireteam slipped past. Pvt Rodriguez nodded as he passed. After returning the nod, Imara turned her back to the door, watching the ragged passage they'd carved through the snow. She heard one muted groan of a floorboard and then nothing else as the second fireteam entered to back up Bowers' team.

Three minutes later, Imara felt movement behind her.

"All clear, Sergeant."

"All, Cummings?" Imara slipped past him and shut the door.

"We checked the kitchen cupboards, if that's what you mean." He proffered a toothy grin.

"We find the electronics Walters was looking for?"

"She's like a kid that fell into the largest T-n-T bag ever," said Cpl Bowers from a door at the end of the room on the left.

Cummings moved, and Imara followed. They passed through a sitting room with clean-lined furniture. A fireplace on the far wall glowed with banked coals.

"Sure the house is empty?" Imara asked.

Bowers nodded and pointed up and then down. "Top to bottom, Sarge. Four floors if you count the basement."

"And the tech?"

"No one was hiding it." Bowers pointed over her shoulder with her thumb.

Behind Cpl Bowers, Imara could see several tables stacked with monitors and metal boxes with blinking LEDs. Cables snaked along the floor under the tables and up two of the walls, disappearing into neatly cut holes. Most of the screens were dark. Of the two that were displaying, one showed the ragged lines of comm transmissions. The second one was a weather map. An overlay indicated where Grabouw and Bhisho were located. The nearest major city was also marked on the map. For it to be in the same frame, the image must have been pulled back a great distance.

"That's a storm," Imara said. She wasn't a meteorologist, but the swirl on the screen was unmistakable. And it was just touching on Grabouw and heading north. They were going to be in it for a while.

"We should hurry?"

Imara turned away. "I don't think we can hurry fast enough. We just have to do our best. Where's Walters?"

Bowers laughed. "In the basement. I think she's overwhelmed."

Cummings led Imara to the basement door. It had been locked, and the lock forced open with less finesse than the front door. Imara went down to find Cpl Larson and Walters in a room stacked with small crates. Most of it clearly labeled as Allied Planets property.

"Wow."

"Those were Walters' exact words. Or word," said Cpl Larson.

"If you wanted to know what's going on," Walters said, "you only have to look at this. A.P. doesn't give this stuff away just to be good neighbors."

"No, they don't," Imara said. "Stuff like this comes with a price."

"I thought the A.P. was hands-off? That the push by the Rhone was their own idea."

"That's what we were told, Corporal," said Imara. She reached for her comm and paused. Unlikely she could raise the ship or her C.O. "Things are definitely not what we were told."

"On the bright side," Walters said as she tapped a box with the toe of her boot, "I found everything we need."

"Then let's get out of here." Imara turned back to the stairs and paused.

At the top of the stairs, Cummings was signaling for silence and more.

Someone was at the back door of the house.

Imara signaled to Larson's fireteam to remain quiet. Cummings had disappeared from the top of the stairs without a sound. What she didn't want to do was wait at the bottom of the stairs while one of her teams faced the unknown without backup. She didn't know if there was a person or a squad or a platoon. As much as she hated it, though, she had to wait for some sort of signal.

Hopefully, it wouldn't be gunshots.

Behind her, Larson and the others had slowly moved close to her. Like her, they were ready to rush the stairs at the first chance.

Upstairs, Imara heard a door lock scrape and click. A knob turned, and a door hinge squealed briefly as it was forced to do its job. A second later, the door shut and the locks were set. Imara set one foot on the first step.

"Who the – !"

A scuffle started, punctuated by grunts of effort. Imara took the stairs two at a time, her steps heavy. The following fireteam added to the noise, sounding like a stampede of Hospitaller orphans being let loose for lunch. At the top, they dashed down the short hallway and took positions on either side of the kitchen entry.

Imara took the first quick peek. She had to take a second one before what she saw registered on her brain. Only then did she relax. She signaled to Larson to stand down his fireteam before she entered the kitchen.

The kitchen was in disarray. Several cupboards had been knocked open. A chair was broken, as were several plates and cups. In the middle of the floor, there was a pile of bodies. Three of them were sitting on top of a fourth. The fifth person already in the room was Cpl Bowers. She was standing by the door, sporting a split lip. Despite that, she was grinning.

"That was fun," she said.

Imara barked a short laugh and then came around to see who their guest was. She knelt as the man twisted to glare back at her. One of his eyes would be swollen shut by the end of the day.

"What are you doing here?"

Imara nodded. "Good question. And I so want to ask you the same thing, Mr. Dmytro Barnes."

13

After a few minutes of hostile cooperation, the Hospitallers had Dmytro sitting in a chair, his arms tied behind his back. His ankles were strapped to the front legs of the chair. Despite Cpl Bowers's disagreement, they had coated the skin around Dmytro's eye with a cooling ointment that would minimize the swelling.

"Don't think I'll thank you," Dmytro said. His arms flexed several times as he continued testing the restraints.

"You don't have to thank us, it's what we do. Aid and comfort," Imara said.

"And defend," Cpl Bowers said. She touched her lower lip with one finger. "Don't forget defend."

"You had that coming," said Dmytro. "You're in my house."

"Your house?" Imara feigned surprise as she looked around. "This can't be your house. You're not from Grabouw. Come to think of it, I don't even think you're from Abira."

"It's still my house."

"Right. Fine. Your house." Imara pulled a chair over and sat facing Dmytro. "Any chance you know who was in the west woods last night?"

Dmytro grinned. It would have made a shark nervous. "I don't know what you're talking about."

"Okay. Why are you here?"

"I live here."

Cpl Bowers stepped forward, lifting one knee. Imara put a hand out to stop the corporal from putting a boot in Dmytro's chest.

"Why do you live here? I thought the A.P. was taking a hands-off position concerning the conflicts here."

"Hands off doesn't mean we aren't interested."

Imara sat back, pushing Bowers back with the same hand she'd used to stop the corporal from giving Dmytro a boot. "So this is a listening post. And I'll go ahead and make the assumption that the forces in the woods were Rhone. I don't think the A.P. government is stupid enough to put their own forces on the ground.

"Arrogance makes people do funny things," said Cpl Larson. He was leaning against the edge of the entryway into the kitchen.

"Arrogant? Like you all? Coming into this house thinking no one would notice?"

"You don't seem to have noticed," Imara said. She kept her face blank as she spoke. They'd known it was possible, but they'd been lucky so far, and the weather had been on their side. Had they tripped a sensor somewhere? She casually signaled for Larson to investigate. He nodded and slowly slid away from the side of the entry and into the hall.

"I'm not the only person in the town. And they've been conditioned to mistrust Hospitallers and to hate them."

Several gunshots echoed through the house.

Dmytro fought his restraints, breaking one arm free. He reached for Imara, who simply slapped him aside as she stood. Dmytro fell onto his face, unable to rock the chair to either side. Imara put a boot on his head. She hated to admit it, but she did push a little harder than necessary.

Several more shots filled the air. Cpl Bowers signaled her team. Cummings watched the back door, Harmon had her weapon pointed at the kitchen window. Bowers and Pfc Sullivan bracketed the door.

"Larson?" Imara asked, her voice loud.

"Company," Larson shouted back. "Took one down and the other two got away. Walters is hurt."

Walters. The one they were counting on to make the landing beacon.

Imara took her foot off the side of Dmytro's face. "If you want to save lives, you might consider having someone call those APCs back to the woods."

"You're outnumbered." Dmytro's growl was slightly muffled by his face being pressed into the floor.

"We'll see." Imara started toward the front of the house. "Bowers, fall back."

In the front room, Pvt Rodriguez and Pfc Schultz were watching the door and windows. Larson was kneeling next to Walters. He had a can of liquid bandage in his hand, the nozzle pressed to Walters' shoulder. On the floor, face down, one of the locals lay dead. An older version of a Dark Worlds' assault rifle a quarter meter from his hand.

"Walters?"

"Grazed me, Sergeant. I'm okay."

"More than a graze," said Cpl Larson. He dropped the can and now had a hand-sized bandage out and was pressing it over the wound and Walters' jacket. "It's a pretty deep furrow. Still, nothing that Walters can't deal with."

"I think it's just an excuse not to carry that box of supplies she's put together," said Pfc Schultz.

"I can still carry it."

"No, you can't," Imara said. She grabbed several parts from the box and shoved them into her jacket. "Everyone load up."

A noise in the kitchen drew their attention. Cummings moved over to the hallway and then moved down with Cpl Bowers behind him. In seconds, they returned.

"He's gone," Cummings said. "He's still got parts of the chair tied to him, though."

"We're out of time, then." Imara pointed at the box of equipment gathered by Walters. "Grab and go. We don't know how long we have. Larson, your team on point. Take Cummings with you in place of Walters."

"I can take point," Walters said. She grabbed the pistol grip of her rifle. The look of pain on her face was impossible to hide.

"I don't doubt you," said Imara. "But you are the only one who knows anything about the landing beacon. You are now precious cargo. Cummings? With Larson, go."

Cummings slipped past, pausing to grab the power source needed for the beacon. He strapped it to his chest as he made his way to the door.

"I can take point," he said.

"You got it," replied Cpl Larson. He turned to the rest of his fireteam. "Rodriguez, me, Schultz. Let's move."

"You're with me," Imara said to Walters.

"I can do something," Walters said. She looked forlorn.

Imara rolled her eyes before grabbing two smaller items from the box and pushing them into Walters' jacket. "Carry those. Don't lose them. And quit arguing."

"Yes, Sergeant."

Imara nodded to Cpl Bowers and then left the house with Walters close behind. Ahead of them, Pvt Rodriguez was looking left down the canyon carved by the locals. Across the gap, Pfc Schultz was watching the other direction. Imara held Walters back while she confirmed the way was clear.

"Rodriguez, escort Walters across."

"I'm not a civilian, Sergeant." Imara didn't miss the growing anger in Walters' voice.

"No, you're not," Imara said. "But you're wounded and have a bigger role now. You have a duty, stay focused on that."

"Come on, Walters," Rodriguez said. He grabbed Walters' forearm and started across. She started to hesitate and then, with a dramatic tilt of her head, pushed ahead, shaking Rodriguez's hand free of her arm.

Imara kept watch while they made it to the other side. Behind her, she heard the soft crunch of boots on packed snow.

"You have grenades?" Imara asked Cpl Bowers, who was now behind her. She was digging a grenade from a pouch on her gear belt.

"Two," Bowers said. "You want me to put one on a timer?"

"Five minutes behind the last of your fireteam. Keep moving."

Imara stepped across the gap and into the rough passage they'd carved on the way in. The falling snow was already collecting at the bottom. How many hours before the whole thing was filled again? As long as the passage remained, it was an easy path leading others to where they were holed up.

Gunfire brought Imara up short. She tapped her comm. "Who's taking fire?"

"Back here," Cpl Bowers said. Her voice was audible through

the comm and behind Imara. "Sullivan's hit. He's okay."

The conversation was punctuated by more shots. Some she recognized as being from Hospitaller MUWs.

"Grenades both ways," Imara said. "See if you can collapse the passage. Then pull back."

"Will do."

Seconds later, the air reverberated with the vibrations of several grenades exploding. The walls of snow on either side of Imara vibrated and slumped a quarter of a meter, sliding down and covering her feet. She kicked the snow off and moved forward, almost colliding with Walters, who was brushing snow off her helmet and shoulders.

"Don't stand too close to the walls," Imara said. "We don't want to lose you."

Additional gunfire turned them both around. Cpl Bowers and Pfc Sullivan were moving backward, weapons aimed in the direction they had come. Sullivan was leaving bright red blooms of blood in the snow.

"Sullivan?" Imara asked.

In response, he held up his left arm. Several drops of blood dripped off in rapid succession. "It's still in there," he said. "Came through the snowbank."

Another grenade exploded. More of the snow slumped, covering everyone's feet. Pfc Harmon appeared, high-stepping through the fresh snow.

"Two down," she said. "They're civilians, though, so it wasn't a fair fight. Grenade moved the rest of them back."

"Let's go then," said Imara. "Sullivan, you're with Walters."

"Yay," Sullivan said as he slipped past Imara. "The walking wounded."

"I'd prefer to see you running."

"Yes, Sergeant." Sullivan grinned at Walters. "At least we didn't take one in the leg."

They didn't run, but they began to move at a lope, kicking the snow as they advanced. Imara trailed after them, Cpl Bowers and Pfc Harmon bringing up the rear. As they progressed through the snowy passage, more gunfire opened up ahead of them.

"Cpl Larson, report," Imara said after tapping her comm. She slipped in the snow, falling to one knee. Bowers gave her a hand up and then continued forward.

"We got company left and right," Larson said. "Some of them aren't civilians. I'd say there was at least a squad of Rhone infantry in town."

"Pop a couple grenades up. Toss a few more down both directions. Do it now."

"On it."

Imara closed the comm and spoke directly to Cpl Bowers. "Drop two on a timer. One now, the second as we cross over the road."

"Will do," Bowers said. She slowed down, waving Harmon to move ahead.

They continued forward. Imara was three meters behind Sullivan and Walters when the first grenades exploded off to the left and right. They were quickly followed by two more. The walls on either side shook, sloughing snow that buried their boots once more.

"Hey, Sgt Fermo," said Sullivan as Imara bowled into him. He managed to keep upright and hold Imara from laying herself out at his feet.

"Why are we standing here?" she asked.

"Waiting for the green light," said Walters. She pointed ahead where Pvt Rodriguez was holding up one arm, his hand a closed fist.

"Stay here," Imara said. She moved forward until she was an arm's length from Rodriguez. "What's the holdup?"

"Cpl Larson," Rodriguez said. He pointed with his chin.

Imara looked across the gap. In the next section of the tunnel they'd forced through the snow, Cpl Larson was standing, leaning into the wall of snow. His rifle barrel was hidden in the snow. His face shield was down, the edge glowing with HUD light. As Imara watched, he was making minute adjustments to the direction and angle.

When he pulled the trigger, someone not far away grunted and fell silent. Larson pulled his rifle out of the snow and turned to

14

The sky was gray with more than just snow and clouds as Imara pushed past the snow that blocked the front door of the farmhouse. The trip through the storm had been slowed by the masses of snow being dumped from the clouds. The passage they'd carved on the way into Grabouw was nearly filled with fresh snow by the time they were halfway back.

Imara had slowed their speed for another reason, too. She didn't want to lose anyone. While it might have been unlikely because of the remnant of their earlier passage, if it were to happen, even she wouldn't be able to find them.

She counted them as they passed over the threshold and into the farmhouse sitting room.

"Eight and me make nine," she said to herself. She gave Cummings a little push to move him further inside so she could shove the door closed. The drift that had begun the moment the door was open required more effort than would typically be needed to shut a door. A snowdrift had quickly risen the open doorway, slumping into the farmhouse.

Imara kicked at the snow and shoved with the door. Cummings returned to assist, and with a final angry puff of snow, the door closed. When she turned around, Imara was wrapped about the waist by several pairs of arms.

"We told you we'd be back," Imara said. She tousled several heads of hair before moving further into the room. "Where's Sullivan?"

Cummings pointed. "Kitchen. Cpl Bowers is going to pull the bullet. If she can find it."

"And Walters?"

"Basement."

"Find Pvt Rodriguez," Imara said to Cummings. "I need you both upstairs and watching out the windows."

"We'll see snow."

"You will, but you may also see movement if you tap into the eyes we've left out there." Jodi rushed over for a second hug. Imara paused while she returned it. Then she gave Pfc Cummings one more piece of information. "We need to be ready. They'll figure out where we went. It's only a matter of time."

"Understood." Cummings paused to tousle Billy's hair and then jogged down the hall. Imara heard his booted feet clumping up the stairs.

Imara paused for several more waist-high hugs and then made her way to the kitchen. "How's it looking?"

Sullivan was sitting on a chair, his arm laid out across the table, his palm pressed against the surface. Bowers and Pfc Schultz had rolled back Sullivan's sleeve. Imara regretted the cut they'd originally made into the sleeve to stop the bleeding. The material was now damaged. Sullivan's forearm wasn't going to get the same protection from the cold.

"It's not in too deep," Bowers said. She had her task light on, and her face shield down. Imara knew that Bowers was using the shield's heat map to highlight the bullet. "Bone's not broken, either."

"Well, my lucky day," said Sullivan.

They each carried a small medkit that included the cans of liquid bandage, several bandages, and topical anesthesia. It would curb the pain, but Sullivan was still going to feel it. In the same kit, they also carried their own body bag as a reminder of what they were doing and the price that might be paid. Imara hoped they would stay sealed in their pouches for another day, at least.

"You're alive," said Bowers. "So, yeah, it is your lucky day."

Imara nodded in agreement and made her way to the basement door. Every time Imara took her squad out, and they all came back alive, she considered herself lucky. Others might disagree with the luck aspect as anyone who knew Imara knew she had become exceptionally aware since Nadia's death.

Cpl Larson met Imara at the bottom of the stairs. This was

Imara's first time down here, and she scanned the area as she returned Larson's nod. The batteries were directly opposite the staircase. To the right were rows of shelves with plastic boxes and totes. Imara judged this as the place they'd found fresh clothes for the children. Past the shelves was a partially open door. That looked like the room where the extra food had been secured until Imara's people found it. To the other side was a machinist's dream.

Walters was there, sitting on a tall stool, hunched over some of the equipment they'd brought back from the mission into Grabouw. She held her right arm close to her side as she worked with a screwdriver. Around her, apart from the electronics that were her responsibility, there was a lathe, drill press, and several other large tools. Tools would be helpful in the maintenance and rebuilding of farming equipment.

"Doing okay, Walters?"

"Doing okay," she replied, her focus still on the equipment she was working on.

"You do know Cpl Larson is here, and you can ask him for help?"

Walters nodded and said, "I do, Sarge. Thanks."

"I tried to help as soon as we got down here," Cpl Larson said. He chuckled, clearly remembering the moment. "She waved me aside and said I was in her way."

That sounded like the mind of a focused person, in Imara's opinion. She'd have to see if maybe Pfc Walters should be considered for specialized training and a new position in the Orphan Corps.

In response to Cpl Larson, and seeming to read Imara's mind, Walters said, "I know what I'm doing."

Imara and Larson chuckled.

"I'll leave you to it, then." Imara clapped Larson on the shoulder before returning to the ground level of the farmhouse.

Pfc Harmon sat with the children in the living room. She was quietly reading a story pulled up on her tablet. She acknowledged Imara with a brief nod that Imara returned. Imara watched the rapt faces of the children listening to Harmon's words. It briefly reminded Imara of Saturday mornings when she was a child. Her dorm father had loved reading stories to Imara and the rest of the squad. He gave every character its own voice, and there was always an outbreak of small voices if he mixed up the character voices.

Those were happy times. But then they'd never been under imminent threat of attack in those days. They could stay here for a while, but they'd have to move eventually. The Rhone weren't going to just let Imara's squad walk away.

Imara turned toward the forest she couldn't see but instinctively knew the direction. They'd go there. All they had to do was find a way to keep the children from freezing to death.

She returned to the kitchen.

"How we doing here?"

Cpl Bowers was wrapping a bandage around Sullivan's forearm. "We got it. It's a bit of a mess. The medtechs are going to give me grief."

"Sullivan? How're you feeling?"

"My arm feels like a dropship landed on it and bounced several times." He lifted his arm and slowly moved it in slow circles. "But I'll live."

"Glad to hear it," Imara said, and she was. "If you'll keep Harmon and the kids company, I need to put the others to work."

Sullivan stood. "I can work, too."

"Good. Work at keeping the kids company with Pfc Harmon."

With a laugh, Sullivan made his way past Imara. "Will do, Sarge. Will do."

"What do you need us to do?" asked Cpl Bowers.

Imara didn't respond right away. She was watching Sullivan join Harmon and the children. He was favoring his bandaged arm. Once he was sitting, she turned back to Bowers. "How bad is his arm?"

"Nicked a tendon," said Cpl Bowers. "And I had to cut in a little more than I would have liked. I'd be surprised if he could hold an idea in that hand right now."

"So we're down one," Imara said. Bowers nodded agreement. As a squad, though, they didn't have time to lick their wounds. They still had work to do. "Okay, then. I need you and Schultz to go through those shelves in the basement. We need either cold weather clothes or lots of layers for the kids. Soon as Walters gets that beacon together, we're moving out."

"Find clothes, you got it," said Cpl Bowers. "Let's go shopping, Schultz."

Imara stepped aside and let the two hurry past. When she heard boots on the steps down, she made her way to the stairs leading to the second floor. She went to the bedroom where she had previously contacted Maj Stewart. Pvt Rodriguez was in the room, near the window. His face shield glowed along the edges, indicating he was using his VR.

"In the room," Imara said by way of notifying him of her presence.

"Hey, Sgt Fermo. You need me to do something else?"

"Not at the moment, Rodriguez. Carry on. Let me know if things change." Imara tapped her comm for Maj Stewart.

Several times she thought she heard someone else's voice over the comm. But the static whispered in fluctuations that could easily be interpreted as voices by anyone who willed it so. The storm, the atmosphere, maybe something more, all of it was wreaking havoc with the comms. It had gone on for several minutes. Before she could decide to keep trying or surrender to the fact contact wasn't going to happen, the room across the hall exploded.

The entire house felt like it had shuddered with the explosion. Pvt Rodriguez rocked sideways and staggered several steps. His helmet hit the window, cracking the glass. Imara had thrown herself sideways, to the far side of the bed, as dust, snow, and debris billowed through the doorway.

"Rodriguez?" Imara asked as she jumped back to her feet.

"I'm good, Sarge. Stay on watch?"

Good question. Was it worth the risk? "For the moment. Be ready to drop out if I need you. Or if the whole house starts coming down."

As if to emphasize her point, a muffled explosion vibrated the house with an intensity far weaker than the previous. Whatever was being thrown at the house missed the second time. Imara hurried, unsure as to how much time they had, and stepped through the debris into the hallway. Overhead, part of the roof was missing. The snow was already drifting in, claiming new territory. The door to the opposite room had swung partially shut at some point. The light coming from the room was as bright as the outdoors. Small snow flurries swirled through the gap, hinting at the state of the walls and roof there.

Imara started across the hall when a shadow appeared amongst the flurries of snow. It solidified into a figure as Pfc Cummings pushed the door open and stumbled into the hallway. Snow hung on him, and a trail of blood led from his nose to his cheek. He looked around and then stopped when he saw Imara.

"Incoming."

"You think?" Imara grinned, glad to see he was still himself. She stepped over to him and then guided him into the other room. Inside, she pushed him to sit on the bed.

"Came out of nowhere," Cummings said. "Heard it just before it hit and managed to hit the deck."

"Mortar?" Imara asked. She was confident it was, but there were several other options.

"Sounded like it." Cummings paused and wiped at the blood with the back of his hand. "Felt like it."

The house shook, the explosion that came with it rattled the windows and knocked dust loose.

"I'd say they got lucky with the first shot and are now trying to figure out what they did right the first time." Imara tapped Pvt Rodriguez on the shoulder. He responded by tapping himself out of VR. "Which means we still have time."

"Sgt Fermo?" The question was shouted up the stairs. It was Pfc Sullivan.

"We're good! Put the kids somewhere safe. Stay with them and send me Harmon."

"Will do!"

"You can stand, Cummings? You operable?"

Pfc Cummings nodded. "Good, now. What's the plan?"

Imara started across the room, heading for the door. "Well, as the roof is now gone in the other room, it seems we have us a firing platform." She stopped and turned to look back at

Cummings and Rodriguez. "So, let's get them before they get us."

They followed her across the hall, joined by Pfc Harmon, who was running up the stairs.

"What happened?"

"Mortar," Rodriguez said. Then, "Are you okay?"

"I'm good, thanks. Sgt Fermo? What do you want me to do?"

In the other room, Imara was already lifting the short end of the bed, tilting it away from the center of the room. "Eyes first. Let's get a picture of the scene. Use thermals. We just need plot points."

While she kicked and shoved debris out of the middle of the room, the other three switched barrels on their weapons and loaded eyes for firing. She used the barrel of her MUW to clear away the remaining jagged edges of glass in the bottom of the window frame. Despite the heating units in her uniform, Imara was already feeling the cold now given free roam of the room with no ceiling and most of the front wall missing.

"We're ready," Cummings said.

Imara looked at the space around her. There was plenty of room for the three to stand and fire. "Eyes up," she said. "When you have targets, switch to grenades. We don't have an endless supply, so don't waste them."

"Will do," said Cummings. "Or won't do, I guess. Will do our job, but won't waste the grenades."

Imara gave Pfc Cummings a pat on the chest. "I trust you to do it right, Cummings. I trust all of you. I'm going to check on everyone else. You go and say hello to our friends out there."

15

At the bottom of the stairs, Imara found Cpl Larson and Pfc Schultz. They were well back from the windows but watching them over the ends of their rifle barrels. Cpl Bowers was in the kitchen, doing the same thing.

"What do we have," Cpl Larson asked.

"Not sure yet. One or more mortars, that's all we know right now. Cummings, Harmon, and Rodriguez are looking now. They'll try to take out what they can, but I wouldn't be surprised if we had company trying to sneak in on the ground floor, too. Where are the children?"

"Basement," Cpl Bowers called from the kitchen. "They're with Sullivan."

"Walters is almost done with the beacon," added Cpl Larson.

"Good. Keep watch. I want to check on the kids. And on Sullivan." Imara took the stairs to the basement, remembering not to hurry. The last thing anyone needed was for her to break her neck falling down them.

In the basement, Walters was in the same position, except she'd put her helmet back on. She didn't see Sullivan or the children.

"Sullivan? Report."

"Back here!"

Imara turned and saw Billy with his toy cat, standing in the doorway to the room where the food supplies had been hidden. She made a shooing motion with her hand, sending him scurrying back into the room.

"Walters?"

"Almost done, Sarge. I'm connecting the power source, and then I need to port in with my tablet and load the beacon protocols."

"How long?"

Walters turned to look at Imara, her face stern, the skin between her eyebrows furrowed. "I need as much time as you can get me."

"We'll do our best, Walters. Just be ready to move when I give the orders. Depending on what's out there, it could come sooner than either of us could want."

"Then I guess I'd better get back to it," Walters said, emphasizing with a curt nod. She turned back to the beacon on the table. Imara thought it looked nothing like the clean-lined boxes with handles on each side. But then, those were made in factories where the workers weren't currently snowed in and taking mortar fire.

Several barely audible thump-noises reminded Imara that they could give as good as get. Cummings and the others were firing back. Things always seemed bright when they could respond in kind.

Imara moved past the shelves and into the small room beyond. The children were sitting on boxes, gathered around Pfc Sullivan, who had his tablet out. As he looked up, Imara caught a glimpse of pictures.

"Showing them where you grew up, Sullivan?"

"Sure am, Sarge." Then, "How's it looking up there?"

"Messy. We're going to evacuate as soon as we get some idea of the forces waiting for us."

"Tell her. Tell her." Casey, the other little boy, was nudging Pfc Sullivan with his elbow.

"That's my bad side," Sullivan said as he adjusted his position to keep the boy from banging against his arm.

Casey stopped moving. His head suddenly seemed too heavy for his neck. "I'm sorry, Pfc Sullivan."

"I'm not mad, Casey," Sullivan said.

"You have to be careful," Cassandra said. She picked up Casey and put him on her own lap.

"I know," Casey whispered.

"Casey's right, too," Imara said. "Tell me, because I have no idea what you are all so eager to say."

Pfc Sullivan climbed to his feet. "Jodi found it when they tried to play hide and seek. Not seeing them made me nervous, and I asked them to stop. Jodi said she'd found the best hiding place."

"I did," Jodi said. She beamed with pride.

"Is this really the time?" Imara asked. She knew Sullivan wouldn't waste her time, not when they were being attacked. But he could be trying to mollify the children.

But Pfc Sullivan grinned and nodded his head. "Oh, I think you'll like this, Sgt Fermo. Jodi, since you found it, you can show the sergeant."

The little girl jumped up and then skipped to the sidewall. "It's over here."

Imara followed the short distance. There were crates stacked here, listing to one side. Jodi disappeared behind them.

"Back here, Sgt Fermo," Jodi said.

With a smile, Imara stepped around the crates to discover another door. This one was open, too. But Jodi hadn't gone in. She pointed at the door from ten or fifteen centimeters away. Imara waved her back so she could slide past the crates and peek past the door with her task light on.

Beyond the door was a tunnel. The walls were cinder blocks. Overhead was a repeating pattern of one concrete and four wood beams. The tunnel went on for some distance. Imara guessed close to fifty meters. She dropped her face shield and tapped on several virtual buttons. The data came back as fifty-one point two five meters.

"Do you know where it goes?" Imara asked Pfc Sullivan.

"Didn't explore it," Sullivan said.

Imara guided Jodi back to the rest of the children. "Good work," she said to the little girl.

"I can guess, though," Sullivan added. "Extreme weather worlds have them. They allow people to access other buildings when it's too hot or cold or wet to be on the surface."

Imara paused as the vibrations of several close explosions distracted the children. She smiled at them when they looked to her for reassurance. To Sullivan she asked, "So you think that leads to another building? I don't recall seeing any."

"There could have been a building," Sullivan said. "An old barn, maybe? But it'd put some distance between us and those people out there. If we can get out."

"If we can get out," Imara said. That was the critical part. If they couldn't, they'd be trapped down there. While she was thinking, she pulled out one of the eyes she still had and the last hand from its pouch. She connected them and carried them back to the tunnel. "We'll gather more data while we see to the enemy. Keep the kids safe."

"Will do, Sarge." Sullivan held up his tablet and spoke to the children. "Anyone want to see the inside of a space station?"

Imara left Sullivan to give the children a picture tour. At the stairs, she checked in with Pfc Walters.

"Almost, Sergeant. Almost." Walters's voice was a mutter of annoyance.

On the ground floor, things hadn't changed.

"No movement that we can see," Cpl Bowers said from the kitchen.

"Nothing on IR, either," said Cpl Larson.

"Keep watching," said Imara. "We're working on a back-up plan."

She took the stairs to the second floor two at a time, mindful of the snow that was beginning to pile upon itself in the hallway. In the bedroom that was missing the roof, Pfc Cummings had his shield down. The glow on the edges indicated he was looking at something besides the room and the other two Hospitallers with him.

"One more," Cummings said. He swiped his hands across the air in front of him. "That's the coordinates."

Rodriguez and Harmon nodded. They turned, and each loaded a grenade. Cummings had turned off his VR and lifted the face shield.

"Hey, Sarge," he said. "Too late, you missed all the fun."

"Fill me in."

"Well, there's one mortar placement left." Cummings paused as Rodriguez and Harmon took aim and then fired. "But IR shows them still pushing forward. Two places. One is in a straight line from Grabouw. The other is working its way around to our right."

"Bodies?" asked Imara. She was interested if two platoons were coming, or two people.

"Looks like fireteams." In the distance, they heard the double bang of two grenades exploding. "That's the last of the mortars."

Imara was about to congratulate the three on a job well done when she was punched in the chest and shoulder several times. The impact was enough to knock her over. A micro-second later, her mind registered the sound of large-caliber rounds pounding holes through the walls.

Everyone was on the ground. Rodriguez was crawling toward Harmon.

"Report," Imara said. She rolled over onto her stomach and regretted it as pain exploded across her chest and shoulder.

The walls were being chewed up in the unrelenting attack. Rounds buzzed over their heads, slapping through the opposite wall.

"It hurts," Cummings said. "Armor held up. But I can feel a nice graze across the ribs and the back of my hand."

"Rodriguez? Harmon?" Imara held her breath, waiting for an answer.

"I'm good," said Rodriguez.

The bullets continued unabated.

"I took one in the leg," Harmon said. "In the meat, I can still move my leg."

"Good," Imara said. "Move to the hall and take the stairs. On your belly, if you must."

"On it," Harmon said. She started crawling towards the door. Rodriguez and Cummings followed.

Imara tapped her comm. "Larson? Bowers?"

"Alive, Sgt Fermo. Large rounds coming in from the west. Fortunately, the fireplace is still holding up."

"Get in the basement," Imara said. She started to crawl to the hallway and stopped. Just above her, bright streaks of light had appeared several times. "Sullivan and the kids have found a possible back door. Drag Walters if you must. She can finish the beacon when we're safe."

"To the basement, yes, Sergeant," said Cpl Larson.

Imara paused a few more seconds, watching more of the tracer rounds flash overhead. She switched her view over to the impact wall. Dark holes, exhaling smoke, dotted the wallpaper. Things were heating up.

"Harmon? Can we get down the stairs?"

"Yeah, but not far," answered Harmon. "Maybe when they pause to reload, one of us can get by, and you don't mind walking through fire."

Imara didn't mind walking through fire if no one was shooting at her. The thought played silently through her head. The second floor had gone quiet.

"They're reloading," Cummings said. He started to his feet.

Imara stood, too. "Back of the house, go now."

In the hallway, Rodriguez was helping Harmon to her feet. Imara pushed them ahead of her.

"Not the bathroom," Imara shouted ahead to Pfc Cummings. "Left bedroom."

Cummings turned and pushed past the partially closed door. Harmon entered next, followed by Rodriguez. Imara had reached the doorway when something burned along the left side of her ribcage. She twisted half around as she fell into the room.

"Down!" She crawled to the far wall as rounds began peppering the hallway and punching through the inside wall of the room.

"They reload fast," said Rodriguez.

"I could have done it faster," said Harmon. She'd pulled out a canister of liquid bandage and was dispensing it into the holes of her uniform, coating and covering the entrance and exit wounds.

"I smell smoke," said Cummings.

Imara agreed. At the moment, she was distracted by the pain along her ribs. It was an awkward angle for looking, but she was able to see part of the line a tracer round had cut through her uniform and her skin. The wound was shallow, seeping tears of blood. She dug out a patch and pressed it over the wound and the hole in her uniform, sealing it off.

"Rodriguez," Imara said. "We need that window open. Can you take care of it?"

He and Imara both watched where the rounds penetrated the room and where they struck an opposite wall. They were moving in slow degrees toward the outside wall and the window.

"Yes," Rodriguez said as he scooted over to the window's ledge. "Open or gone?"

"Gone is fine." The way the house was being torn apart, what damage the Hospitallers did to it would go unnoticed.

"I see smoke, too." Cummings was pointing to the doorway. Billowing in swirls of motion, gray smoke was moving towards the back of the house as if it might also be seeking egress.

Rodriguez was on his feet. He jammed the window with the butt of his rifle several times. The glass shattered, most of it clattering and tinkling as it fell outward. When most of the glass was gone, he used the barrel to break away the jagged teeth still caught in the frame. Once it was gone, he grabbed the vertical frame pieces that bisected the window and yanked at them until they gave way. He tossed them out the window.

"All clear, Sarge," he said. The line of bullet holes was expanding, now touching the outside wall. Light flickered in the hallway as smoke began to roll into the room.

"Okay, Hospitallers," said Imara. "We're going out the window. There's no time for niceties. First one out goes far left. Everyone else makes their own hole. Stay off each other."

"Will do," said Harmon as she clambered to her feet. She'd left the liquid bandage canister and a small pool of blood on the carpet. "A little help, Rodriguez?"

Rodriguez helped her onto the ledge. She turned and looked like she was about to say something when the hallway exploded. The concussion knocked her out the window.

"Sounds like they found another mortar," said Cummings. "You wanna hurry up, Rodriguez? Your girlfriend's waiting."

"What? Hey, she's –."

"Not now, Rodriguez!" Imara shouted. "Jump."

Rodriguez jumped. Imara looked at Cummings.

"I should have kept my mouth shut. Sorry, Sgt Fermo."

"Just keep it shut until we're back on ship. Now, your turn."

Another explosion shook the house. Pfc Cummings took a

running jump, going out the window head first. Imara crawled to the window on her hands and knees, mindful of the broken glass. Her gloves would keep her from cutting herself. Still, it would cut the gloves. She could already feel her uniform losing some of its heat-generating ability.

At the window, she stood and then climbed onto the sill and paused just long enough to identify where the other three had gone into the snow. Then she jumped.

16

Everywhere around Imara was the gray-white of snow of late day. She also had snow in her helmet, under her chin, and in one ear. It was colder than she'd expected and jolted her more than a pot of hot Insta ever could. When she looked up, causing a small cascade of snow to wash across her face, she could see the opening she'd made about a meter overhead.

The waning day was being pushed back by the yellow light of an active fire. There hadn't been a mortar explosion since Imara had jumped. The machine gun firing had also finally stopped. The heat from the fire would soon melt the nearby snow, though, exposing anyone too close.

"Check in," she said. She moved her arms and feet, compacting the snow and giving her more space to move.

"Behind you," said Pfc Cummings.

Imara turned to see Cumming's face poking out of the wall of snow behind her. He had a smile going.

Rodriguez, his voice muffled by walls of snow, replied, "Alive and well."

"Good here, too," said Harmon. Her voice was the most distant of the three.

"No more injuries?" asked Imara. She could just imagine, as she'd done on her way down, of someone impaling themselves on a fence post.

"The cold feels good on my leg," Harmon said. "But that's a problem, isn't it? I shouldn't be feeling the cold."

"No. Neither should I. Cummings? Rodriguez?"

"I've got a couple cold spots, too," said Rodriguez.

"Toasty here." Cummings was still grinning as he pushed snow aside, opening the space between him and Imara. "So, now what,

Sarge?"

"Now, we go and join the others." She hoped she hadn't doomed them. But now there was the benefit of someone digging them out from the top if they had trouble digging up from below.

Through the snow, Imara could hear Rodriguez chuckle.

"You losing it, Rodriguez," asked Cummings.

"What? Oh, no, no," answered Rodriguez. Imara could hear the humor in his voice. "I was just about to ask how we were going to find them. Then I remembered who we're with."

"Gotcha." Pfc Cummings turned to Imara, snow sliding down his face shield. "So, which way, Sarge?"

The tunnel entrance under the house was more west than where Imara stood. They would have to converge on the spot just above where the tunnel ended. Imara knew the distance to travel. Maybe there would be a building there. Likely there would be a wood pallet covering the exit.

"This way," Imara said. "Rodriguez, Harmon? Follow my voice, but let's keep the volume down."

Imara started pushing through the snow. She used her hands and feet to push and kick the deep but soft snow aside. Once the snow settled in, they'd need shovels to dig through. Hopefully, they'd be long gone from the surface of Abira before then.

Behind her, Imara could hear the heavy breathing of the others as they pushed aside any snow that fell with Imara's passing. They had put Harmon between Rodriguez and Cummings since she was sporting a leg wound. Further back, Imara also heard the crackling and popping of wood burning. She wasn't sure why the Rhone soldiers or people from Grabouw hadn't surrounded the farmhouse. Maybe they hadn't had enough people. Or maybe they'd assumed no one could get out. Or maybe they were surrounding the farmhouse even now, and Imara was getting her people away just in time.

Would it be enough in time? She still had to retrieve the rest of her squad and the children from the tunnel end.

"Need me to take over?" Cummings asked from behind.

"Not yet," Imara said. "We're almost there. "Then, we'll all have to search for the entrance…"

Imara stopped. Her left boot had struck something made of wood. It wasn't a log. It felt more like a plank. She bent down and scraped away the snow that was dark gray and dirty looking. Removing the snow revealed a burnt strip of lumber. Imara scraped away more snow until she uncovered a thick upright, burnt to a stump.

"I think we found the barn," said Imara.

The others had pushed forward to join her.

"Someone burned it down?" asked Harmon even though none of them could possibly know the answer.

"Looks like it," Rodriguez answered anyway.

"So the tunnel should come up here," said Imara. "if Sullivan was right. We just have to figure out where."

"Could we call them?" asked Cummings.

Imara laughed. She'd been too occupied with just finding the others with her amazing sense of direction and forgot one of the more straightforward solutions. She tapped her comm, reaching out to connect with Cpl Bowers or Larson. When the connection was made, she gave Cummings a thumbs up.

"Sgt Fermo," Cpl Bowers said. "You make it out okay?"

"More or less. Harmon is wounded. Rodriguez is battered. Cummings is Cummings." Imara paused while the people around her and Cpl Bowers laughed. "What about the rest of you? Everyone get out?"

"We did," said Bowers. "We had to drag Walters from the workbench. I think she finally saw reason when an overhead beam crashed onto the stairs."

"The kids?"

"Bundled up and relatively okay," Bowers said. "Whole situation is kind of scary for them. Are you here?"

"Think so," Imara said. That seemed funny to everyone around her. "We could use a clue, though."

"We may have that for you, Sarge. Just a second."

The comm crackled. Then, Cpl Bowers was on. "Hey, Sgt Fermo," he said. "Schultz and I managed to pull down several boards that were part of a trapdoor. There's a lot of debris on top, but I shoved an eye up to the surface. You can zero in on it."

"Yes, we can." Imara signaled Cummings, who touched his helmet to bring his VR online. "Be with you shortly."

"Roger that. Oh, and Walters wants you to know she has the beacon working."

"Tell her I said, 'Good work.'" Imara cut the comm and then turned her attention to Cummings. "Found it?"

Cummings pointed. "That direction." He laughed and added, "Is this what if feels like to be you, Sarge?"

Imara found herself laughing, too. Then, she gave Pfc Cummings a little push. "I wouldn't know. Get going."

"Follow me."

Cummings began to push a new tunnel through the snow. Imara sent Rodriguez next before directing Harmon to follow. She followed after Harmon, listening back the way they had come. She still heard the fire devouring the farmhouse. But she also thought she heard several voices coming from the same direction.

Tapping the comm for a general connection that would include her entire squad, she said, "Whoever attacked us is still active and nearby. So, voices low and only when necessary."

Rodriguez and Harmon looked back in Imara's direction and acknowledged her with a thumbs up each.

They pushed through the snow for another minute and then Cummings came to a stop. He knelt and pushed snow aside with his hand. When he stood, he was holding one of the Hospitaller eyes. As he turned to display his find his right leg disappeared into the ground, taking the rest of him to the ground.

The first thing Imara heard as she went over to help him was muffled laughter. "I think they got you, Cummings."

"That they did," said Cummings. "I'm sure it was the kids' idea. My own people wouldn't betray me like this."

"No, no, of course not," someone said from down below. "We Hospitallers are a serious group."

"All right, everyone," Imara said as she helped Cummings stand as he cautiously pulled his foot free. "We need to dig out and get moving."

It took fifteen minutes to clear the opening and ten for everyone to safely exit. Imara made them take another ten minutes to replace the trapdoor and push debris and snow back on top. Once the snow started to fall, which was likely at any moment, their work would be hidden.

"Looks like the fire is still going strong," said Cpl Bowers.

"Might be why the Rhone haven't moved," said Cpl Larson. "It'd be toasty warm near the fire, versus how cold it is out here."

"Who has damaged heaters?" Imara asked. The bullet that had grazed her side had also cut the heating elements in that part of her jacket. Heating elements near the wound could only compensate for so much before the cold seeped in. It would also drain the power cells faster.

"I do," said Sullivan.

Everyone but Cpl Bowers and Pfc Cummings raised their hands. Most of those who did had small cold spots. Harmon and Sullivan had entire limbs without heating to protect them.

Imara waved Cpl Bowers and Cpl Larson over. "And the kids? How are they going to be?"

"We have them in triple layers," said Cpl Larson. "Except for the shoes."

"There weren't any," Cpl Bowers added. "All they have are the shoes they came with. But we put adult socks over the shoes. That should help some."

The children were gathered with the other Hospitallers. Cummings and Rodriguez were making small snowmen to entertain the children. She'd have to remind them to knock them down before they left. There'd be no denying their presence if the Rhone came upon them before falling snow could provide camouflage.

"That will have to do for now. Maybe we can find one of the summer cabins that are supposed to be in the hills."

"What about the beacon?" asked Cpl Bowers.

"We can't go out there," said Imara as she pointed in the direction of Bhisho. "Not until we have the kids somewhere safe. So, that's our first goal. We take care of that, then we go and put out the welcome mat."

"Sounds good," Cpl Larson said. "Let's get going. Where's the forest, Sgt Fermo?"

Imara pointed. "It's that way. Everybody up. Cummings, disperse the snowmen."

Cummings convinced Billy and Vanessa to give the snowmen a good stomping, and then they were ready to go. Imara put Pfc Schultz on point and followed close behind. Cpl Larson and Pfc Walters followed with two of the children. Then came Pfc Cummings, followed by Harmon and two more of the children. Sullivan preceded Cassandra. The remainder of the Hospitallers fell in behind with Cpl Bowers bringing up the rear.

Pfc Schultz plowed through the snow, pummeling the soft powder with her arms. She forced an opening through the snow that was adding layers now that the snow was falling once more. Imara knew Schultz couldn't keep the pace she'd set for very long. When she saw Schultz hesitate for a breath, she called Pfc Cummings forward.

"Wait for Cpl Bowers," Imara told Schultz.

Pfc Cummings proceeded with the same aggressive energy. It occurred to Imara at that point that they were trying to get clear of the snow for the children. For their part, the children appeared to be taking the trek well. They were quiet but stayed with the Hospitallers nearest them and didn't slow down, not becoming a drag on the rough march toward the forest.

For their part, Imara heard several of her people quietly praise the children for their efforts. That seemed to keep the children as warm as the activity was.

They continued on. Imara noticed the chill seeping into her side. She was grateful for the distraction of Rodriguez's exclamation of triumph. He'd only been at the front for several minutes when he brought them out of the three-meter deep snow. It sloped away quickly, ending at several trees deep into the forest.

Imara reminded the children to remain quiet even as she was filled with a desire to shout with relief. They'd spent so much time in the deep snow that she was beginning to feel like the remainder of her life was going to be spent cold and covered in it. There was still snow on the ground. Even the trees couldn't keep out what was falling in relentless abundance. But here it was less than half a meter deep. Overhead, though, the branches of the trees were bent with an ever-thickening burden of fresh snow.

"Now all we have to do is find one of those cabins we've heard so much about," said Cpl Bowers as she knocked the snow off her boots.

"There's likely a road," said Cpl Larson. Then, "I know, everything's covered in snow, but roads are wide and flat."

"And no trees," Imara said. "Yes, I think that we can move uphill until we find it. We'll give it fifty to seventy meters before we move northeast."

"Which direction is that?" asked Cummings.

Imara pointed without hesitation. "That way."

"Of course it is." Cummings shook his head. "Why do I ask?"

"Because you like to see her point," said Cpl Larson. "Who's on point?"

"Wait." Harmon limped over to where Imara and the two corporals were standing. "I swear I'm not asking for myself, but maybe we could use a small breather?"

"You didn't have to ask," Imara said. "I think we could all use a small break. Break out some rations, make sure the kids get something to eat. Make sure you get something to eat."

"You setting the example?" asked Cpl Bowers. Her arms were crossed over her chest. Her chin had a slight upward tilt of defiance.

"Don't I always?"

Everyone within hearing laughed. Imara shooed them away as she fished a ration pack out of a side pocket. It was warm enough from the uniform's heating elements to be palatable. The children seemed to enjoy the rations more than any Hospitaller ever did. They sat on a log that had been wiped clean of snow and munched happily on fruit and nut bars. Bars that had been manufactured long before any of them had been born.

Imara made sure that the children and her people saw her eating, and she glowered at anyone that attempted to avoid the same fate. She was just finishing the last bite of her protein pack when deep booms vibrated the air, knocking a layer of snow free from the tree branches.

"That what I think it is?" asked Cpl Larson. He'd started brushing the giggling children free of the new dumped snow.

"The Rhone attack on the rest of our company?" Imara oriented towards Bhisho. The town was in the same direction that the noise originated. "I think that's what it is."

17

While she folded and tucked away the wrappers from her rations, Imara walked another ten meters along the tree line. Relative to the actual distance to Bhisho, it wasn't far, but it gave her time to think. They needed to get the beacon out into the fields, close enough to the battle so it would be effective.

At the same time, they couldn't bring the children with them, and they no longer had time to go hunting for one of the summer cabins. So, what was she going to do with the children?

As she mulled over her situation, Imara continued listening to the boom of small artillery and mortars. Once more, she tapped her comm, hoping for an open line. She didn't believe she could raise Maj Stewart, but she would be negligent in her duties if she didn't try. The comm crackled unusually.

"Bowers, Larson!" She turned and marched back to the others, meeting the two corporals halfway. "Try your comms. Ping someone you know that should still be in Bhisho."

They both nodded and tapped their comms. Cpl Larson turned ninety degrees, and Cpl Bowers tilted her head in the act of listening. They both stayed that way for more than a minute.

"That's not normal static," said Larson.

"Jammer?" asked Bowers.

Imara nodded. "My thoughts, too. But jammers aren't cheap to make or operate."

"Maybe they got one as a Founders' Day present," said Cpl Bowers.

"I doubt they celebrate Founders' Day," Cpl Larson said.

Founders' Day was the celebration of the establishment of the Hospitallers. On that day, the children of all the orphanages were treated to special presents as part of the celebration.

"I doubt it, too," said Imara, smiling as she noticed Bowers's eye roll. "But if their jammer is strong enough, it'll interfere with the beacon."

A rolling rumble of artillery vibrated the air, dropping several branches and a blanket of snow.

So, now they had three objectives to accomplish. The first two Imara already knew about. Keep the kids safe and deploy the beacon. Now they also had to find the jammer and disable it. There was no longer any time to mull over her options. Action was now required.

"CSMO people."

There wasn't exactly a shop to close. Still, they policed any garbage that might have escaped during their hasty meal. After a few sips of water, they were ready to move out.

"Fifty meters through the forest," Imara said. "Parallel to the snow line. Then we turn."

She put Pfc Cummings on point and followed behind him. Cassandra had moved to catch up and took Imara's hand. She gave the girl a quick smile and a hand squeeze, but she didn't pull her hand free.

"You okay?" Imara asked.

"Cold," Cassandra said. "But now that we're moving, I'll warm up. We did jumping jack competitions in the house to stay warm. Before you all showed up."

They weaved past several trees. Mortar fire was a distant whisper. As they walked, Imara watched the roots and fallen branches broken from the trees by dense layers of snow. "Who won?" she asked.

"Billy won a lot, except when he was too tired from winning. Or, when one of the little ones looked sad that they couldn't win."

Overhead, something cracked. Imara pulled Cassandra backward as a branch fell in a micro blizzard of snow. They walked around it, taking long strides to recover their place behind Cummings.

"Did it bother you to lose?" Imara asked. "I'm assuming you lost all the time."

"I didn't need to win," said Cassandra. "I needed everyone else to stay warm and positive."

Imara nodded. Cassandra might be too old for the regular orphanages. Still, there would definitely be a place for her in the Paladin forces if she were so inclined. If they couldn't find a family on Abira that would take her.

The conversation and dodging several more falling branches kept them occupied until Cummings raised his hand and balled it into a fist. They'd covered fifty meters. Now they had to set the children up until they could return.

"I don't think Sullivan or Harmon should come," said Cpl Bowers.

She, Cpl Larson, and Imara had convened to discuss the next part of their plan, such that it was.

"They're not going to like it," said Cpl Larson. "But Sullivan can't fire a weapon, and Harmon's leg is slowing her down."

Larson pointed back the way they came. Harmon, who'd insisted on taking the rear guard position, was just now joining the rest of the squad.

The artillery fire was coming at random intervals, which didn't vibrate the tree branches as much.

"Right," Imara said as she pulled her attention from Harmon and back to the impromptu meeting. She agreed with the assessment of the two corporals. This was her squad, though, and she would have to make the call and deliver the bad news. "Snowstorm's gotten worse, too. This is not going to be pretty."

Imara's next meeting was with Pfc Sullivan and Harmon. Neither of them was completely surprised by Imara's decision.

"Everyone's going to be slow in that storm," Harmon said. Her defense was obligatory. Imara knew Harmon was aware of her own condition and how she could be a distraction to the rest of the squad if she faltered.

"I'd say I could still use my other hand," said Sullivan. "But I also know I'd likely be a hindrance. And someone does have to stay with the kids. With Harmon's help, we can build a quick lean-to, cover it with snow for camouflage, and keep everyone warm."

"We'll have to take turns on lookout," Harmon said. Distant artillery thunder underscored her statement. "We can't assume anyone won't come along."

"Good, I'm glad you two have this covered. Sullivan, scout a location. Harmon, stand fast."

Sullivan nodded and walked away, scanning the ground around them. There were now plenty of branches on the ground and increasingly more snow.

"Harmon," Imara said, her voice low. "I don't know if there are feelings between you and Rodriguez. If there are, understand that I will do my best to keep everyone alive. But you also know that death happens."

"I'll apply for transfer as soon as we're back on the ship," Harmon said. Imara noticed Harmon's gaze flit to Rodriguez's direction and then back.

"Let's step through that airlock when we get to it, okay, Harmon?"

"Yes, Sgt Fermo."

Imara tilted her head and, with little nods, pushed Pfc Harmon's attention to her left. "Looks like Sullivan has found a spot. You should gather the kids and start helping."

"On it, Sergeant. And thank you." Harmon limped in Sullivan's direction, whispering loudly for Cassandra and the other children.

Imara watched them for several minutes. Behind her, she could hear movement as the rest of her squad moved about, talking softly. Daylight was coming, but the sky was still dark. Snowflakes continued to find their way through the treetops. At random intervals, the crack and thump of branches breaking and then slapping the ground punctuated the otherwise silent atmosphere. She closed her eyes and soaked in the silence while it existed. Soon, things were going to change.

When she heard the crunch of approaching footsteps, Imara opened her eyes and turned. Cpl Larson was approaching.

"Hey, Sarge," he said. "They seem to have taken it well."

Imara spared a glance for Pfc Sullivan and Harmon. They had the bones of a large lean-to going. The children were bringing branches and layering them across what would soon be the lean-to's roof.

"It's because they still have responsibilities," she said. "If I'd told them to sit here and twiddle thumbs, they'd have been justifiably frustrated."

"I'll file that away under 'useful leadership tips,'" Larson said. "What about the rest of us? We don't want to be frustrated."

"Unload anything you don't need. The T-n-T bags, extra rations. That kind of stuff. Leave them with Sullivan and Harmon. We're going to go put out the welcome mat. And then go turn it on."

The snow in the Saastal valley was either different from the snow around Grabouw, or the weather had changed for the worse. Pfc Schultz had been pushing the beginning of what Imara expected would be a two-kilometer long tunnel. In less than forty meters, the tunnel became a canyon.

The snow had been falling for weeks, based on the information that Imara had. In most places, it was still soft fluff they could push through. But snow had weight, and it pushed down on the snow beneath, pressing it together. Out from the trees, the lower layers of snow had become packed enough that it could be walked on.

That was how Imara found herself standing in a slope of snow that only reached to her armpits. But now they had to deal with winds that reached forty kilometers an hour whipping snow up off the ground, mixing it with that which was still falling.

Schultz backed up until she was in the deeper snow. She pulled up the collar of her jacket that was fitted with a gas filter but worked well as a muffler against the biting wind.

"I thought this place was cold enough before," said Schultz as she pushed the filter mask up over her nose. She flashed a thumbs up and pushed back into the opening and the hard blowing wind across the cold, white land.

Imara followed, serving as the compass. The local comm was also disrupted by the Rhone jammer. To alter Schultz's direction, Imara had to raise her voice to be heard over the wind or tap on Schultz's shoulder. This meant that instead of a single person on point, there were two.

Worse, Imara noticed that the snow was beginning to fall faster and thicker. Certainly, it would mask their presence, but it also meant they couldn't spread far apart. They had to bunch up, making them an easier target if they were seen. Imara pulled Schultz to a stop and waited for the others to come closer. She pulled them into a huddle, their helmeted heads touching, blocking some of the sounds of the wind.

"Weather's getting worse," Imara said. "We'll need to stay close. You should be kicking at the heels of the person in front of you. If we hit white-out conditions, you can't fall back. We lose you even for a moment we may as well have lost you forever."

"Understand, Sarge," Cpl Bowers said. "Stay close. Like when we were in elementary grades and walking down the hall."

"That close?" Rodriguez asked as he pinched his nose shut. Then, "Ugh, good thing the wind's blowing hard. Eh, Cummings?"

There was general laughter followed by Cummings tossing a hastily made snowball at Rodriguez's face shield.

"All right. Cummings, you take over for Schultz. Remember, stay close."

After a general acknowledgment from everyone, Cummings moved to the front. Imara was close behind. She looked over her shoulder to verify that Cpl Larson and the Pfc Walters were on her heels. Larson nodded and then checked over his shoulder.

"Go now?" Cummings asked.

Imara nodded, "Go now."

Cummings started forward, pushing away the top half-meter of snow as he went. Several times there was a deeper drift. They tunneled through just as they had in the fields around Grabouw. The pace slowed at those moments, and the time under the snow was a small respite from the frigid wind that seemed to be picking up speed.

If there was any positive at the moment, Imara would have said it was the absence of artillery and mortar fire. This might be the Rhone's world, but that didn't mean they knew how to fight in these conditions. Imara didn't think anyone really did. Like her, she was pretty sure the leaders were making it all up as they went along and hoping that it worked.

A half-hour passed by the time Cummings came to a sudden stop. They were in complete white-out conditions now. Imara found it almost impossible to determine where the snow in the air ended, and the snow on the ground began. She came to a stop with her hand against Cummings back. She felt the pressure of Cpl Larson's hand on her back.

"Cummings? You need to be relieved?"

Cummings turned sideways. "No, Sarge. I'm good. But there's a wall in the way."

When they'd first landed outside Bhisho, Imara had noticed the long ridges of snow. She only knew they were hedgerows and stone fences because she'd seen the images sent to her tablet that showed the same land in the summer. What the snow did not reveal, and what she only knew from those images, was that there were gates in every wall and hedgerow.

So, all they had to do was find the gate.

First, Imara did a count. "Pass it back. Count off from the rear."

Larson nodded and repeated the command to Walters, who repeated the process. Thirty seconds later, Larson tapped Imara on the back.

"Five," he said.

Imara turned to Cummings. "Six."

"Seven," said Cummings. "Now what?"

"Go left." If they didn't find the gate, they'd reach another wall. At that point, they'd climb over.

Cummings pointed left and then started forward. Imara felt the pressure of Larson's hand on her back ease and then return as he moved to keep with her. While Cummings continued to serve as a human snowplow, Imara stuck her free hand out, searching for the wall. She scraped her knuckles against it before she knew it was there. It was almost a relief to contact something of substance in a world that appeared to be absent of everything. It was much like being in VR without a program running.

Minutes passed before Cummings stopped once more.

"I found the gate," he said over the sound of the wind.

Imara moved closer to Cummings until she too felt the wood

planks. Behind her, the hand on her back remained in constant contact.

"Now, if we can get it open," said Imara. The snow was deep on both sides.

"If you want," Cpl Larson said from over Imara's shoulder. "Or, we can just go through it. I doubt it's built to withstand a Hospitaller boot."

"Good point." Imara hated destroying civilian property. But she reminded herself that the Rhone, with their artillery, were doing far worse to Bhisho. "Go on, Cummings, makes us a hole."

"You got it, Sarge."

It took four kicks to clear enough space through the gate for everyone to pass. They stepped through slowly, Imara directed Cummings on a slight angle to the right to bring them back on target.

Before they moved, Imara turned once more to Cpl Larson. "From the rear, Larson. Count off."

The command went down the line. When Cpl Larson tapped Imara's back, his eyes were wide. "Four," he said.

It was math so easy, a United Planets Marine could do it. Imara was now number five. Cummings became number six. Someone was missing.

18

Imara grabbed Cummings and pulled him back until he was next to Cpl Larson. She moved Larson's hand to Cummings' shoulder and then stepped down the line, sideways. She kept one hand on Larson as she moved.

"Walters," Imara said. "How's our beacon?"

"Good, Sarge."

"You know who's missing?" Imara had moved her hand from Larson to Walters as she sidled along the line.

"Rodriguez."

The pit of Imara's stomach was suddenly a hard knot that echoed an ache of personal pain. She nodded and moved down the line until she reached Cpl Bowers. Cpl Bowers looked as pained as Imara was feeling.

"What happened?"

"I lost him for a second," Bowers said. She waved at the ground. "I stumbled on something. A rock or something. My hand came off him for a second, no more. It wasn't until you sent back for a count and Shultz turned to me instead of him."

"Shultz," Imara said. "You didn't feel Rodriguez let up on your back?"

"I did, but then it was right back. I assumed it was still Rodriguez."

"How long ago did that happen?"

"I tripped before we went through the gate," Bowers said. She looked sick.

This wasn't like losing someone in a firefight. They'd all dealt with that kind of death since they left basic training. But in those times, their squadmate was dead. They could see them and knew what happened. In its own strange way, there was closure. But losing Rodriguez in the snow was unfamiliar, an unknown. Add to that the general fear of freezing to death alone. Then add to that Imara's promise that she was bringing everyone out of this mess alive.

"All right. Hold hands. You're the anchor Bowers. We're going to sweep and hope we scoop him up. Then I'm volunteering him for kitchen duty back on the ship. For a year."

Bowers and Schultz clasped hands. Imara moved back down the line toward Cummings, relaying the same orders. She stepped between Cummings and Larson, holding their hands as she moved into place.

"Cummings," Imara said. "Start walking. The rest of us are the rope. Do not let go. You understand?"

"I understand."

They swept a circle with a radius of ten meters. Three hundred square meters covered out of tens of thousands. A drop in a bucket. And no Rodriguez for their effort. He could have been separated from them by the wall. He could have come through but then lost contact. Imara snorted a laugh. He'd probably stopped, intending to help Cpl Bowers to her feet.

"We can't keep looking," Imara said to the gathered group. "The rest of the company is at risk. As is the entire town of Bhisho. I'm sorry."

"We're all sorry," said Cpl Bowers. Imara was certain Bowers felt even worse.

"If he stays to the walls, he might make his way to the town, or at least be safe until the storm passes." Cummings spoke loudly, but it didn't mask his doubt.

"We all know the risk," said Imara. "Now, keep in contact, don't let go. Another kilometer. We're almost there."

This time, Imara took point. Pfc Cumming's hand gripped at the suspender of her utility belt. Cpl Bowers followed with Pfc Walters behind her. Cpl Larson was at the rear. Imara took a breath and let her senses point her to the spot she'd chosen for the beacon. It was where they'd dropped in just a few days ago. A few days that were supposed to be dull days of supply distribution.

Imara moved forward, taking several slow steps. Once she fell the resistance of Cumming's grip, she pushed forward a little faster. Her mind, despite locking onto her destination, still managed to flutter with conflicting thoughts and emotions. She knew moving forward was the right thing to do. At the same time, she felt like she was deserting Rodriguez.

The ghost of her decision pushed Imara forward. Yet, always she was mindful of the other four Hospitallers chained to her. The path was not a straight line. A deserted henhouse diverted them for a meter, and then a hedgerow. Imara tore her way through the hedge, using some of her frustration to fuel her actions. Then, the next half kilometer had been a long slog, kicking away the piling snow to clear the path, keeping her chin tucked in to keep the snow from being blown under her face shield by the wind.

Finally, she stopped. There were no landmarks to reassure anyone else as they huddled together around Pfc Walters, who'd dug a hole in the snow and set the beacon inside it. She was now fussing over the power source and adjusting two dials that hung on exposed wires.

Walters waved Imara down to her.

"There's not a lot of power," she said. "But if they can get even one dropship here, the others will be able to lock onto their position."

"But...," said Imara. She'd raised her eyebrows for emphasis.

"But we have to knock out the jammer," said Walters. "And we have maybe a couple of hours. I'm not sure if I can guarantee much more than that."

"We have to find the jammer," Imara said as she stood. She raised her voice. "I'd thought we could pop an eye up and see what we got on the heat map."

"In this weather?" asked Cpl Larson. "I'm not sure a bonfire would register through this cold."

"Exactly," said Imara. "They'll keep it in the rear, for safety. If we used the sound of artillery and heavy gunfire as a mark, I can guide us just south of that. Then we'll have to get lucky."

"Or," Walters said as she stood up in the middle of the huddle, "we could just triangulate on the jammer."

"We could?" Cpl Larson asked.

Imara's mind was working out the logistics. Walter's simple comment had revealed an idea Imara had forgotten was possible. "Yes, we could. But we need to spread out north to south."

"Far apart," said Cpl Bowers. She looked around in a meaningful manner. "We'd be out of contact with each other."

What she meant, in Imara's opinion, was that they could lose someone else. Or lose everyone.

"We could use a wall," Walters said. She held her hands out, wide. "Keep to a wall, spread out, no one moves until Sgt Fermo brings us back in."

"We'd need a wall," said Cummings. And then he looked at Imara.

All of them looked at Imara. Cpl Bowers grinned as she did.

"What? You all think I know where a wall is?"

"No," said Bowers. "But we think you know in which direction to find one."

Of course she did. She might not know where every wall and hedgerow in the fields were, but she had studied enough to know that if they went west, they'd hit one soon enough. And the clock was ticking.

"Line up," Imara said as she stepped through the huddle past Cpl Larson. "We don't have time to waste."

The storm had swirled its way from white-out to hints of a cloud laden sky back to white-out in the twenty minutes it took to find the wall. Imara found it next to her without realizing she'd found it. There was a bit of disorientation as she realized its presence. She'd been about to comment on her lost ability to navigate blind.

"Still ninety-nine point nine percent perfect," Cpl Larson said as they huddled up.

"Let's hope that point one percent doesn't happen today, then," said Imara. She tapped Walters on the shoulder. "You stay here. I'll move the others down the wall. Start collecting data."

"You got it, Sarge," Walters said. She turned and put a hand on the west wall and then leaned against it while she started up her VR to manipulate the virtual controls.

"Everyone stays in physical contact until I place you," said

Imara. She moved, and the others came with her. Ten meters and she put Cpl Larson at the wall. Pfc Schultz was left in position ten meters along. Ten meters more, and she left Pfc Cummings.

She and Cpl Bowers continued. They stopped after ten meters for Bowers, but also because they'd found another gate. The gate unlocked. They dug out around it until they could pull it open enough that they could slip through it later. Imara gave Bowers a thumbs up and moved further down the wall. She reached ten meters and paused for a moment before continuing another ten. It was a long shot, hoping that Rodriguez would appear, but she still hoped.

Now that hope had been extinguished once more, Imara turned her attention back to the task. She fired up her VR and then her comm. Unsurprisingly, the comm wasn't working, overwhelmed by jammer static. She adjusted the comm band, narrowing it and then turning her head, letting the static rise and fall in volume. She did this for several minutes.

Imara's mind drifted as she collected data. Again she thought of Rodriguez and the promise she'd made to Harmon. Those thoughts took her to Nadia, which brought her hand to the two pocket knives pressed together. Not every Hospitaller seemed inclined to form deep relationships. They were all like family. Most of them played around, but they also seemed to avoid serious relationships. Someone had told Imara that it had a lot to do with their origins. It was also why many of them chose sterilization after turning twenty-five. There were those, and she'd met a few, who did marry, who did have children. But often they were also people who hadn't served in the Orphan Corps

When Nadia curled up, her back against Imara's abdomen and chest, they'd talked of children and lives outside of the Orphan Corps. There were plenty of other jobs they could still do as Hospitallers. Jobs that would allow them to have a family. Those dreams had ended with Nadia's death. It had never occurred to Imara to undergo sterilization before. But now, she had the paperwork on her tablet.

The tablet reminded Imara that they were being jammed. That told her that she still had a job to do. That brought her attention back to the VR scan she'd been conducting.

Five minutes. Way more data than they needed. The others were probably wondering where she'd gone. What would they do without her? What was she going to do without Nadia?

Imara shut down her VR, closed the comm, and hurried along the wall to the gate and then to Cpl Bowers across the gap.

"You had me worried," Bowers said.

"I had me worried," said Imara, though not so loud as to invite a response. "Grab on, let's go."

Imara moved back down the wall, collecting Cummings, Schultz, and then Larson. She gathered them all together, into a tight huddle, at the spot where Walters waited.

"We didn't need that much data," Walters said. She was moving and twisting her hands on controls seen only in her VR.

"That's on me," Imara said. "Transfer data to Walters."

They were all quiet as they manipulated the unseen controls to send their scan data to Walters. Walters would process it with an overlay of the maps. She worked at it for several minutes after all the data had come to her.

A message light winked on the inside surface of Imara's face shield. Message received. She looked to Walters, who nodded. Imara nodded back and then opened the message. She now had a general location within fifteen meters of the jammer.

All they had to do was get there.

With everyone holding on to each other, Imara led the way back to the gate she and Cpl Bowers had found. The snow had already filled in the space where they'd pushed the gate open. Imara brought Cpl Larson to the point and let him kick a passage through before she pointed him in the direction of the jammer. She made sure they were all holding on and present before she gave Larson the command to move.

Imara was concerned about the time they had. The cold would slow down the drain of the beacon's power source, causing it to last longer. But it could also stop it from working entirely. Walters had assured her that the electronics inside generated enough heat to overcome the cold. She shouldn't have assumed that she was the only one filled with a sense of urgency.

Clearly, Cpl Larson was aware of the time, too. He moved fast enough that Imara stumbled several times over the lumpy, hard snow beneath their feet. She had to tug on Larson's equipment harness to slow his pace.

Four times Imara brought the team to a halt and did a count. It was simple, counting to six, but each time they did, it also reminded her that she'd lost someone. It reminded her in some ways of the wall in the Maj Stewart's office on the ship. Every name of every Hospitaller who had served and died as part of the company since its formation was etched there. The purpose there, much like Imara's count that ended at six. It was to remind the commanding officer of the price of leadership.

Nadia's name was on that wall. As were the three names that were the result of Imara's past inattention. Imara had promised herself there'd be no more of that.

"How you holding up?" Imara asked Cpl Larson during their fourth count. She could see his face was red with exertion. "Maybe we get Cummings on point, and he can yell at the snow?"

Her joke was in reference to Pfc Cumming's tendency to talk too loud for almost any situation. Though, she had to admit, he'd had it under control ever since they'd slipped out of Grabouw.

"I'll do it," Cummings said. "Though I don't think the snow here cares about what any of us have to say."

"Good point," said Imara. "Speaking of 'point.'"

"You got it, Sarge," Cummings said. He crossed the tiny space of the huddle. "By your leave, Cpl Larson."

"All yours." Larson stepped aside, letting Cummings move past.

Imara latched on to Cummings. Cpl Bowers came next with Walters, then Schultz and Larson bringing up the rear.

"Don't wear yourself out," Imara said as Cummings began to shove his way through the snow.

Cummings battled the snow for fifteen minutes before Imara pulled him to a stop. They kicked out enough space for a small huddle. Imara knelt, and the others imitated her. They were out of the wind. She looked at them, one at a time, assuring herself they were all okay. The cold spots on her own uniform felt like they'd gotten larger. The others were all likely dealing with similar uniform issues.

"Okay," she said. "If we've done everything right, we're here."

Walters nodded agreement. "Now, all we have to do is find it."

19

Though time was ticking, Imara made everyone choke down a ration bar and some water. Walters' water had frozen. Imara shared hers. It would do no good to move Walters' water around as it would just suck heat from her, which had the potential for being catastrophic for Walters.

Imara was already short three from her squad. She wasn't going to risk any of them to hypothermia.

When everyone had eaten, Imara got them on their feet. She jogged in place for a twenty count, hoping to drive some heat to her side where the cold was biting at her. Schultz and Walters did the same. Pfc Cummings was doing deep knee bends.

"We're going to go in a zig-zag," Imara said. "Bowers on point for five minutes on a straight line. Then, Schultz moves forward, and we zag on a straight line for another five. We keep going until we hit something, or we move past the area we'd triangulated."

"Not to be a downer, Sarge," Cummings said. "But what if we don't find it?"

"We'll find it," Walters said before Imara could respond. "I know it."

Imara laughed. "Okay, Walters," she said. Then, to the group, "Just be ready when we do. We can't see a meter in this snowstorm right now. But it could slack off and expose us in a heartbeat. If things get busy, try to keep together."

"Will do, Sarge," said Cpl Larson. The others nodded agreement.

"All right, then. Cpl Bowers, go find us a jammer to destroy."

Once more, they held onto each other and began pushing through the snow. The snow, as if to display how unreliable it could be, eased off a little. Imara was able to see just past Bowers who had taken out her t-tool and was using its spade to push the snow aside. So, she saw the Rhone guard the same time as Bowers did.

The Rhone had his back to Imara's team. Bowers held her t-tool back for Imara to grab. She then stepped forward, raised her rifle, and slammed the butt of it into the base of the soldier's skull. He folded and collapsed, rolling forward into the snow, leaving a tunnel where he fell.

Bowers checked the body, signaling to Imara that he was dead. When she stood, she held up a rope.

"Where do you think it leads?" Bowers asked. She had a grim smile on her face. None of them enjoyed taking down the enemy this way.

"We're about to find out." Imara handed Bowers her t-tool. When it was secured, Imara motioned them forward.

Bowers had to let her rifle hang by its sling as she guided the team along the rope. This time, there was no surprise when the next Rhone soldier appeared. And he wasn't alone. There was a yelp of surprise from the Rhone as two of them began lifting their rifles. Cpl Bowers dropped the rope as she threw herself to one side.

Imara fired the moment she had a visual on the Rhone soldiers. The first two went down with two short bursts from her weapon. The third was able to get his finger on his trigger before Walters dropped him with two rounds. The fourth Rhone returned fire. Imara felt the sting along her arm. She reciprocated with her own rifle fire.

The air around Imara vibrated with rifle fire as Cummings and Larson fired on the fourth Rhone. The Rhone staggered back several steps, tripping over the snow pushing against his calves. Collapsed backward, leaving smears of red along the snow as he fell.

By Imara's feet, the snow was pink with diluted drops of blood from her arm.

"Everyone else?" Imara asked. She turned slowly to take them all in with a look.

"I'm going to need a new face shield when this is over," said

Cummings. His shield was cracked just to the outside edge of his right eye.

Bowers, who was climbing back to her feet, looked angry. Imara held up a hand to stop everyone from talking. She signaled for them to look around. The fight had been brief, but in those moments, the falling snow had thinned. Imara could see the dead and all of her fireteam.

She also heard shouting.

"We still have that rope?" Imara asked Cpl Bowers.

"I think so." Bowers searched the ground and brought the rope back up. "Yep, still got it."

"Move. Everyone be ready. Things are going to get hot."

Bowers led again. Imara was right behind her with Cummings holding on the right and Larson doing the same on the left. A quick glance showed Walters had a hand on Cummings. Walters, next to Larson walked sideways to keep an eye on where they'd been.

There were more shouts. This time they came from behind.

"I found it!" Bowers's words were loud with excitement. Perhaps too loud as gunfire began to slice through the snow from several directions at once.

Imara felt a bite on her shoulder as she went to her knee, pulling the others down with her. Cummings, Larson, and Walters were returning fire.

"Walters," said Imara. "Grenades."

Imara left Walters to make the change on her weapon, replacing the standard barrel with the grenade launcher and its short, broad magazine. Bowers had her weapon pointed at a door. It was white and only visible because of the hinges, doorknob plate, and a sign that said 'authorized personnel only.' It was on the back of a large white box several meters tall and four long. The box sat on the back of a tracked vehicle.

"Try the handle!" Imara backed up next to Cpl Bowers. She returned short bursts of rounds. She didn't have solid targets, she could only aim in the general direction. The helmet had IR, but the snow and air were both below freezing. Plus, there was so much snow that nothing would register. It was like playing tag in the dark, blindfolded.

"Locked." Bowers grunted and then fell, bumping into Imara. She apologized as she rolled away, leaving her own blooms of blood in the snow. "Sorry, Sarge. I can't believe someone shot me in the back."

"How bad?" Imara dropped the magazine from her weapon and slapped in another one. She tried to look around Bowers to see her back. Snow flurried in between them, but there was blood visible about midway down the right side of Bowers's back. "You can breathe okay?"

Bowers fired off a short burst. "Felt that," she said. Then, "I don't think it went far. Lucky shot. Just burns, which I guess makes a nice change from all the cold spots I'm feeling. What about the jammer?"

"Stand by." Imara sidled forward to reach the group of Larson, Cummings, and Walters. They'd pulled several of the bodies to them, building a low bulwark. "Everyone okay?"

"Cummings's helmet is down. Good for nothing more than protecting his skull."

"I like traditional," Cummings said. "Oh, and a ricochet caught my neck, just under my ear."

Several rounds burned tunnels through the nearby snow. There were several hushed, but meaty smacks as the bodies in front of the Hospitallers absorbed more of the rounds.

"Anyone else?" Imara asked.

"I'm good," Schultz said in between pulls on her rifle's trigger.

"Caught one in the leg," said Walters.

"I've been buzzed a couple times," added Cpl Larson. "How about you and Bowers?"

"So, just another day," said Imara. "Walters, how sure are we that this vehicle behind us is the jammer?"

Walters fired off a grenade at a low angle that put it almost immediately through the piled snow. She sat back on her butt and tapped her helmet. Not far away, the grenade exploded, highlighting the snow in that direction and collapsing the bullet tunnels. She tapped her helmet once more.

"Cummings, can I have your grenades?"

Cummings fired a burst of rounds and paused to remove two magazines of grenades, passing them to Walters. Walters loaded one and then did an awkward version of a sit-up. She fired a grenade into the snow to her right, where there seemed to be a concentrated amount of return fire.

"It's the jammer, Sgt Fermo. I'm positive."

The grenade exploded, silencing some of the gunfire coming from that direction.

"If we take out the dish and antennae on top? Will that be enough?" Imara winced as a bullet buzzed her forearm. There was now another hole in her uniform, but fortunately, it was only a graze. The cold would ease that pain soon enough.

"It wouldn't be enough to help the beacon," Walters said. "We have to get inside."

"Do we have to turn switches or just destroy everything?"

"Turning off switches would be good, if we can keep the jammer when this is over. Techies would probably think it's Founders Day if you gave it to them."

"Stop it, don't break it. Got it."

Imara moved back to where Bowers was firing down one side of the Jammer. "I think they know what we're up to," she said as Imara joined her.

"Keep them back. We have to get inside and try not to break too much."

"What's the fun of that?" They both ducked as a small burst of fire hit the tread near them. "I think they've figured out exactly where we are. Might want to hurry."

"Pull back," Imara said. "Add a couple grenades to the mix. Walters is having some success with that."

Imara moved back and studied the door. It was a basic lock. She knew a couple Hospitallers who could open it with several pieces of wire in seconds. She wasn't one of them, though. However, just opening the door might not be enough. Not if someone was inside. The door was going to have to come off.

The magazine in her rifle was half gone. She set the selector on full auto and pointed it at the area past Cpl Bowers. "Duck, Bowers."

Bowers ducked.

Imara unloaded the magazine in the area she imagined the Rhone shooters were located. Several shouts of pain indicated she'd either gotten it right, or someone had stubbed their toe hard.

"Keep firing, Bowers."

"I'm on it, Sarge," replied Bowers. She punctuated the end of her sentence with a grenade launch in the same direction.

Imara moved to the other side of the jammer so she wasn't firing across the door. If she did it right, the door would fall open, dropping off the opposite side. Once in position, she dropped the expended magazine and pushed the next one into place. She left the selector on full auto and aimed at the door hinge. It was three quarters the length of the door. She started at the top and began firing, stopping to readjust her aim or when a round pinged off the top of her helmet.

Two-thirds of the way down the hinge, Imara's plans changed. She paused to load another magazine when the door burst open, swinging on the remaining third of the hinge. Two soldiers filled the gap and began firing wildly at a downward angle that shredded the snow three meters away. The door had twisted on the remaining section of hinge, partially blocking Imara from their view.

She still had the magazine in her hand. She scooted forward, still using the door for cover as she loaded the new magazine and seated the first round. As she stood to fire at the two soldiers, she realized they'd turned away from her, toward the opposite side. The side where Cpl Bowers was located.

"Hey!" Imara yelled as loud as she could and then brought her weapon up, setting the butt of the stock to her shoulder and taking aim.

Both soldiers turned, firing as they did. The door still provided some protection, catching most of the rounds meant for Imara. She fired in return, holding the trigger and unloading half the magazine into the two soldiers. One toppled out of the jammer box. The other fell backward, his finger still gripping the trigger.

Imara felt the bite of several rounds in her right shoulder. Her right hand lost its grip on her weapon. It fell from her hand, dangling by its strap. She grabbed the pistol grip with her left hand, raising the barrel to point at the jammer doorway.

"Bowers?"

"Couple nicks, Sarge. You?"

"I'm hurting," she said. Maybe it wasn't as bad as it felt, but if it was, she wouldn't be clearing the jammer box. "Can you clear the inside of the jammer?"

"Stand by."

Around them, the air and the snow still stirred with the buzz of passing bullets. Every few minutes, there was a nearby explosion as Walters continued to launch grenades at the snow-hidden enemy.

Imara tested her hand by squeezing it into a fist.

"Nope, that's not good," she said to herself. She could barely curl her hand without the pain burning white-hot.

She looked over to check on Cpl Bowers. Bowers was standing, her back to the box. She looked in Imara's direction and nodded before tossing an eye through the door of the jammer. Once the eye had bounced inside, she squatted and tapped her helmet. The edge of her face shield glowed blue as she used the VR to study the inside of the jammer box.

Off to Bowers's side, the snow darkened in one section. Someone was pushing closer. Bowers was in VR and unaware. With the grenade barrel still attached to her weapon, she wouldn't have been able to offer up much of a defense.

Despite the pain in Imara's other arm, she aimed her weapon with her good hand. Her aim went wild as she pulled the trigger, throwing the end of the barrel skyward. Despite that, she seemed to have caught whoever was there because the shadow suddenly dropped. Imara kept her eye on the area she'd fired into in case whoever she shot was only wounded, or pretending.

"Hey, Sarge," Bowers said as she tapped her helmet. "There's just the one body inside."

"Get inside. Find an off switch." Imara stepped forward and fired several more times in the direction she'd seen the dark shape.

Next to her, Bowers was clambering up the stairs into the jammer box. Imara took Bowers's earlier position. Out in front of her, Cpl Larson and the others were still returning fire. The snow around them was speckled with dots of blood that were turning pink as they were diluted by the falling snow.

Imara's comm beeped. She ignored it at first, not sure she'd actually heard it. When it beeped a second time, she almost shouted with joy. She had to let go of her weapon to tap the comm.

"Bowers?"

"It's off."

20

The jammer was off. Imara resisted shouting for joy as it would have included pumping the air with her fist. Now, somewhere in the snow, a direction that Imara instinctively knew, the beacon had flipped on. The ship needed to know the beacon was active.

"Good work, Bowers." Imara flinched as several bullets slapped the jammer box near her head. She squatted and tapped her comm, hoping that everyone else was still alive.

"Sgt Fermo?" Major Simmons sounded incredulous. Imara didn't blame him.

"Yes, Major. How're you all holding up?"

"We pulled back from the town before the Rhone forces got into position," the major said. "They're making a mess of the place with their artillery. They attempted a couple of exploratory excursions, but we rejected those pretty quickly. You responsible for the sudden access to comms?"

"Not me directly," Imara said. She paused to fire several rounds into the snow to her left. A dark form threw itself sideways. "Walters built a beacon and found the jammer. Bowers turned the jammer off."

"Beacon? Stand by." The comm clicked. Imara hoped that Maj Stewart was contacting the ship. "Bowers? You okay in there?"

"So far," Bowers shouted back. "The Rhone seem disinclined to damage the interior."

"Keep low anyway." Imara redirected her attention to the other three. "Larson! Pull back to the jammer. Drag your defensive shields with you."

The defensive shields were the bodies of the Rhone dead. Imara had a feeling they were going to need all the defense they could get.

There were only six of them, and everyone seemed to be wounded by this point. Imara had no idea how many Rhone soldiers were out in the snow, unseen. Fortunately, they were as blind as Imara's squad. Each group pulled their triggers, aiming into the falling snow, unsure if they'd hit their target.

But Imara also knew that the amount of ammo her squad possessed was dwindling quickly. And there seemed to be no end to the amount of ammo the Rhone could hurl at the Hospitallers. The Rhone had, after all, come prepared.

Imara tapped her comm. She managed to pull her trencher tool free before connecting with Cpl Larson once more. "If you can send Schultz ahead, I could use a hand as one of mine isn't working."

"Sending Schultz now," said Cpl Larson, "and we'll be pulling back as well."

Imara cut the comm and adjusted her t-tool so that the blade was at ninety degrees to the handle. Then, she began to hack at the snow, one-handed. She did her best to ignore the bullets that were slapping the sides of the jammer, ricocheting off the ladder and occasionally poking her armor. She was trying to dig out the snow from underneath the stairs, near the closest tread. It was a lot of work, especially when every single swing caused a jolt of pain in her other arm.

"You want me to take over?" asked Pfc Schultz from Imara's side."

"No, Schultz, I want you to get your trencher out as well, and we'll both dig. But you can dig faster."

"I'll do my best not to embarrass myself," Schultz said as she reached for her own t-tool.

Imara returned to digging. Schultz joined her a few seconds later after slinging her weapon. Together, ignoring the bullets, they dug as best they could. At one point, something bit Imara in the thigh. She paused for a second, until the initial jolt of surprise-pain passed, and then she continued to dig. There was nothing she could do about any of the bullets that would hit her except for maybe to not let them actually get that far.

A minute after that, several more people emerged from the

dense snowfall. Cpl Larson appeared with Pfc Cummings and Pfc Walters. Each of them was carrying or dragging a body with them.

Imara pointed with her tool. "Drop them there. Make a wall. Then help us dig out this foxhole. We'll need plenty of room for the five of us."

"What do you want me to do?" Cpl Bowers had to shout to be heard from inside the jammer.

Imara shouted back as she hacked the snow one-handed. "Stay down. You have a body in there. Get behind it." She paused to catch her breath and added, "While you're at it, search for ammo, because I don't know how much we have left."

"Not much," said Cpl Larson as he dropped the body he'd been carrying and began to shift the four corpses into position, forming a quarter circle wall.

"That's my fear," said Imara.

Cpl Larson began to rifle the pockets and pouches of the dead. Cummings and Walters continued to return fire at the unseen forces. Imara and Schultz returned to digging out more snow.

Imara stopped at one point, her t-tool dangling by her side. "I can't dig with one arm anymore."

"That's fine, Sarge," said Schultz. "Stand back and let me at it."

Schultz seemed to relish the hard work and threw more snow out at a rapid pace. Imara, unwilling to stand around and appear useless, began stacking the ammo magazines that Cpl Larson was pulling from the dead Rhone.

When the Hospitallers began manufacturing their own weapons, besides making them useful for a multitude of purposes, they also made the receiver and barrel a single millimeter larger than was standard across the second radial arm. That made the Hospitaller ammo useless to everyone else but allowed the Hospitallers to use the enemy's ammo when necessary.

"Cummings," Imara said. "Get in here, now. Shultz? Can you start digging under the jammer's undercarriage?"

Shultz nodded and shifted her position, throwing out more of the snow as she pulled it from under the back end of the jammer. Cummings fell awkwardly into the foxhole. Walters leapt in beside him.

"Cummings? Are you clumsy or hit?"

"I've never been that clumsy." He shifted to a kneeling position and tapped the back of his helmet. "How's my helmet look?"

Imara took a quick look. There was a small dent and a spider crack. "You'll live."

"Oh, good," said Cummings as he climbed to his feet. He joined Walters at the wall of the foxhole and returned to randomly shooting at the enemy still hidden by the falling snow.

"Here's the last of it, Sgt Fermo."

Imara turned to receive the last six magazines that Cpl Larson had liberated. She shoved them, one at a time, into the wall of the foxhole next to the others Larson had collected. "Hopefully it'll be enough."

"Enough for what?" Cummings asked as he ejected a magazine and shoved another into the receiver slot.

Cpl Larson had also set a fresh magazine in his weapon. He then joined the others at the wall, firing over the bodies that were now taking the punishment.

"That should be enough," Imara said, tapping Schultz on the shoulder. Shultz had been in a mental zone, jabbing snow, flinging snow, repeating.

"I was going to dig us a trench all the way home," said Schultz. She closed and stored the trencher. "Another time, then."

There was little that Imara could do but pass ammo and encourage the others. They continued to fire sporadically and in a variety of directions to convince the Rhone that approaching would be a mistake. What she didn't know was how long they would have to do this, or how long they could.

"You getting a message?" Bowers asked with a shout from inside the jammer.

Message? Imara focused on her face shield. She did have a message, but it couldn't be Maj Stewart as it was on a general broadcast for any Hospitaller within range. She felt a rush of adrenaline as she tapped her comm. "Rodriguez?"

"Ah, I was hoping to surprise you."

"Believe me, we're surprised."

"Wait. Rodriguez?" asked Cummings as he continued to aim

and shoot, aim and shoot. "Figures he'd show up after all the hard work was done."

"Where is he?" asked Cpl Larson at the same moment Imara asked Rodriguez the same thing.

"About fifty meters out, hugging the snow. I was trying to bellycrawl my way toward the firefight when the comm suddenly started working."

"We turned off the jammer," Imara said. Though, she realized that it was obvious after she said it. The pain and cold must be getting to her.

"That's great." Rodriguez sounded relieved. "If you could all stop shooting in my direction, I'd like to come in."

"Rodriguez misses us," Imara said loud enough for everyone to hear. They replied with noises of pity. Meanwhile, Imara scanned for Rodriguez's location, now possible only because the comm was available. "He's off the jammer's five. Let's leave him a window to jump through."

The other four in the foxhole adjusted their direction of fire.

"Bowers," Imara shouted. "Don't shoot Rodriguez when he arrives."

"Wouldn't think of it."

"Okay, Rodriquez," Imara said. "We left a window open. Come straight at us, don't deviate."

"Straight line. Here I come."

"He's on his way," said Imara as she tapped the comm closed.

The others nodded and continued to fire. Imara passed a magazine to Pfc Cummings.

"I see someone," Bowers called from inside the Jammer.

"Don't shoot them," Pfc Cummings shouted back.

Imara saw them, too. The dark shadow seemed to extract itself from the snow, separating itself from the thickly falling flakes. Rodriguez had been right to not approach until he could contact Imara. None of them would have known who was racing toward them and would have fired without hesitation.

"It's him," said Pfc Shultz.

Rodriguez was now only several meters away. Imara, too, recognized the way he ran. There was still plenty of gunfire, so

Imara didn't know when Rodriguez was hit. She saw him stumble and then stagger before flopping onto the snow just outside of the body barricade.

Cpl Larson jumped up and out, his torso lying across the bodies. He grabbed Rodriguez and pulled him into the foxhole. They fell into a heap at Imara's feet.

"I think I got shot in the butt," Rodriguez said.

Larson flipped him over. There was a red smear across one side of his left buttock.

"They barely grazed you," said Cpl Larson.

"Probably just used it as an excuse to stop running," said Cummings. He punctuated his words by throwing a small snowball at him.

"We still have an enemy to deal with," Imara reminded them. "Let's get back to the walls."

They were all moving when several things happened around them. Imara realized as they were all moving back to defend their position that no one was firing at them. But the air wasn't just filled with the incessant whisper of falling snow. Instead, there was a distant, familiar roar that was beginning to override the sound of the snow.

"Dropship?" asked Pfc Schultz.

"Yes," Pfc Walters said.

"Dropships, plural," said Imara.

"I gotta say," said Cpl Bowers from the jammer, where she no longer had to shout, "that happened sooner than I would have expected."

Imara agreed, but she wasn't about to argue with the effect. The arrival of the dropships seemed to have had an impact on the Rhone's enthusiasm.

"Not just dropships on the move," said Cpl Larson. He pointed into the snow.

"Aw, are they taking their ball and going home?" asked Cummings.

Large shapes were moving past the jammer, indistinct through the haze of falling snow. But Cummings was right, they were moving in a direction opposite of Bhisho.

Imara resisted the urge to sag to the ground. Partly because she was the squad leader, and it wouldn't be good leadership. Partly because the ground was cold. She was already cold enough in a dozen spots on her body. No need to add her butt to the list.

And then Rodriguez was shouting. "Something's happening!"

What was happening? Imara looked around, confused. Rodriguez wouldn't repeat the obvious they'd all acknowledged. He'd seen something else. Then, Imara saw it, too. "Bowers! The jammer's moving."

"It is? I'll see what's going on."

"Hurry up," said Cpl Larson. "We're running out of room down here."

As the jammer continued to rotate on its axis, it cut off half of the foxhole, rolling over the bodies of several of the dead and began to compress the snow on the edges. The foxhole was collapsing. Walters and Schultz had yanked out their t-tools and were digging as fast as they could, trying to create more space.

Imara stepped away from the work, feeling helpless as she was unable to lift a trencher with her hand. The amount of space beneath the jammer was decreasing. Imara considered crawling out to at least give the others room to work. Maybe she could keep ahead of the rotating track treads.

"There's a driver," Bowers said.

Imara paused in her decision making and shouted back, "Take care of them!"

The jammer continued to turn. Imara could see the others were getting nervous. Then, there was the sound of two shots fired, and the crawler stopped turning. A shadow appeared to the side of the treads near the front of where the crawler had been initially facing. Imara assumed the shadow was the driver.

"Hey, they've got a heater in the cabin," said Bowers.

"That's nice to know, Cpl Bowers," said Pfc Cummings. "But we're kind of stuck down here."

"Right, sorry. Stand by."

A few seconds later, the jammer began to rotate back toward its original position. The jammer had scraped the surface with its treads, pushing shoveled snow back into the foxhole. The weight of the jammer had also caused parts of the foxhole walls to start collapsing. For all their work to dig their way in, they now had to dig themselves out.

"Schultz. Walters. Rodriguez," said Cpl Larson. "Start digging us a way out of here."

The three shifted positions to the rear of the crawler and began shoveling the snow up and out as best they could with the limited working space. Cpl Larson turned his attention to Imara.

"Doing okay there, Sgt Fermo?" Asked Cpl Larson.

"I've been better," said Imara. "But that's only because I normally have two hands that I can use."

Imara could see Cpl Larson studying her. Not that she blamed him. She had a feeling she was a mess. Blood had been leaking from the two wounds in her arm and shoulder. It had frozen on the outside of the uniform, cracking as she moved, but she could still feel a cold wetness underneath.

"You haven't plugged those yet?" asked Cpl Larson.

Imara shook her head and then wished she hadn't as it caused a wave of dizziness to wash over her. Without asking, Cpl Fletcher stepped forward and rummaged through Imara's equipment until he found her medical kit. From the bag, he removed two of the small cans of liquid bandage.

"I'd tell you this is only going to hurt a little bit, but you already know that."

"The freezing cold has helped numb most of it," said Imara. She had a feeling frostbite was going to be a problem, too, when this was all over.

Cpl Larson shook his head and said, "It's still going to hurt."

21

In fact, it hurt more than Imara had expected. Cpl Larson had to pull the uniform material away from the wound. The material had frozen to the skin and blood. Pulling aggravated the bullet entry, leaving Imara to grit her teeth to keep from barking in pain. But once the material was out of the way, Cpl Larson popped the cap off of the liquid bandage canister and pushed the tip into the wound. He pressed the button on the bottom of the can. Liquid bandage flowed into the wound, stopping the bleeding, and numbing some of the pain that remained.

"How does that feel?"

"Better," acknowledged Imara.

The same process was repeated for the second wound, though it took a little bit more effort to locate the actual point of entry. Pulling the material away this time was a bit worse than the first time, too, despite having the experience.

While Cpl Larson had been taking care of Imara, the other three had managed to dig them out from under the jammer. They climbed out, pulling the bodies aside as they went. Once out, they turned around and began helping Cpl Larson guide Imara to the surface. Cpl Bowers came down from the cabin of the jammer and joined them at the back. Imara was compelled to sit on the stairs that led to the jammer box. Through the snow, she could see the shadows of more vehicles traveling past them. She wasn't the only one who noticed.

"That looks like a lot of vehicles," said Cpl Bowers

"Right, I'm thinking they must have had a battalion," said Cpl Larson.

Imara had been studying the shadows, too. She recalled the images through the eye, from when they'd spied the Rhone forces in the forest. She'd thought that looked like a lot, but this was even more.

"I didn't realize there were so many soldiers for the Rhone to bring to a fight," said Pfc Cummings.

"Their population is only a quarter of the planet," said Imara. "But they're more aggressive than the Serdoban. And they seemed to be motivated to win this revolt that they've begun."

"They would've destroyed the town," said Pfc Walters. "If we hadn't been able to activate the beacon."

Also convenient was the nearly immediate presence of the dropships. Dropships that just happened to be ready to come down as soon as the jammer had been deactivated and they could latch onto the beacon's signal. "I have a suspicion," said Imara, "that if we were to open the backs of those first dropships, we'd find little more than supplies, if even that."

"So you think that they had some ships on standby as a scare tactic?" asked Cpl Larson.

"Beats having a bunch of us just sitting in space waiting to drop down," said Cpl Bowers.

Something else was bothering Imara. She knew where Pfc Sullivan, Pfc Harmon, and the children were. She could also see the direction of travel the Rhone were taking. It was possible, purely by coincidence, that the Rhone could roll right towards the shelter the wounded and children were holed up in. The idea of Harmon's wounds and Sullivan's compared to her own cause a giggle to bubble up.

"Are you feeling okay?" asked Cpl Bowers.

"Yes and no," Imara said. "I was thinking of a problem that we have, and my mind sort of drifted."

"What problem?"

Imara shifted her gaze to Cpl Larson. "I'm worried that the Rhone might hit the woods near Sullivan and the others and possibly endanger their lives."

"Do you want us to contact Maj. Stewart?" asked Cpl Bowers.

"Even if we contacted him, he doesn't know where they are," said Imara. "They have their comms off for security reasons."

"And if their comms are off," said Pfc Walters. "If we were

closer, we could ping them on a general comm."

"But we're not," Cpl Bowers said.

"There's nothing else to do but go for them ourselves."

"You're in no condition to make another forced march, Sgt Fermo," said Cpl Larson.

Pfc Cummings reached out and slapped the side of the jammer. "Well, we do have a ride. And the inside of the cab is heated."

"Why walk when you can ride?" asked Cpl Bowers, grinning.

"You sound like the Allied Planets Marines," Cpl Larson said.

"Can I call shotgun?" asked Pfc Schultz.

After several laughs and a shove in the shoulder from Pfc Walters, they all looked to Imara.

"Who's driving?" Imara said. "I have a bad arm."

As it turned out, Cpl Larson had lots of experience driving the RapReps and some of the trucks the Hospitallers used when they were at base. He took the wheel, and Pfc Shultz got her wish to ride passenger. Everybody else made themselves as comfortable as they could in the jammer box. They'd been able to reattach the door, using the guide rope that had led them to the machine. Even so, the cold air and snow managed to find their way through the cracks, so that even with the cabin heater turned to full blast, it was still close to freezing where Imara sat.

Imara cradled her arm, trying to protect it from the jostling and pounding as the jammer rolled across the countryside. It rolled over hedgerows that gave way under the weight of the vehicle. The stone fences were a different matter, but the jammer rocked its way up and then down as it passed over them.

As they progressed, Imara gave adjustments to Cpl Larson when she felt the vehicle deviate from the correct direction. Pfc Schultz was giving an occasional play-by-play as she noticed some of the other Rhone vehicles through the still falling snow. Just once did Cpl Larson have to pull hard on the steering wheel to avoid colliding with another vehicle. It had been traveling perpendicular to the jammer's path. The collision would have put an end to their rescue attempt.

Imara wasn't able to restrain the gasp of pain when her shoulder bounced off the under-counter cabinet behind her.

"The forest is just ahead, Sgt Fermo," said Pfc Schultz. "Hang in there."

"Harmon and the others are more to our left," said Imara from her position on the floor of the jammer box.

The jammer slowed as Cpl Larson eased off of the accelerator. Imara could feel it changing directions to match her comment.

"Do you think we can comm them now?" asked Pfc Shultz.

"We're close enough," Pfc Walters said. "What do you think, Sarge?"

Imara nodded her head. "You can do the honors, Walters," said Imara.

Even if the Rhone were to latch onto the signal and investigate, the rest of the squad would be there to defend the children and the other wounded.

Pfc Walters made the call over the comm. While Imara watched and listened, she was partially distracted by the throbbing that had returned in her arm

"Okay, Sarge, I informed Pfc Harmon that we are coming and what kind of vehicle we are driving."

"I'd say this is all looking familiar," said Cpl Larson. "But it all looks like woods to me."

Imara shifted around, trying to get to her knees. She was having a hard time because of the one arm. Pfc Cummings slid over to assist her. Once Imara was high enough to see through the windshield, she began to give detailed course corrections to Cpl Larson. While Imara was not an expert on forestry, her sense of direction provided her the edge she needed to help guide the jammer until Pfc Schultz spoke up.

"Oh, I know right where we are. Turn left just past the third tree over there, and then we're less than ten meters from their location."

"Left after three, then stop," said Cpl Larson. "You got it."

The jammer turned left as directed by Pfc Schultz, scraping the tree as it turned. Imara smiled as she saw Schultz glare at Cpl Larson over his too sharp maneuver. They rolled forward a few more meters before Larson lifted his foot off the accelerator and applied pressure to the brake. Slowly, the jammer rolled to a stop.

The only noise now was the throaty sound of the heater fan and their own breathing. Imara's comm beeped. Pfc Cummings reached over and tapped the connect button for her.

"Sgt Fermo," said the voice on the other end. "There is a vehicle just outside of our shelter."

"That's us, Pfc Sullivan," said Imara. "We've brought you a ride back to Bhisho."

The interior of the jammer box was not intended for a squad of armed soldiers and a half dozen orphans. The twins and Billy sat up front with Pfc Schultz and Cpl Larson. In the back, Cassandra sat next to Imara, helping to cradle her arm. The other children sat on or close to the other Hospitallers, everyone trying to stay warm. The heater in the cabin of the jammer seemed to have given up its efforts to warm the entire space just prior to the vehicle leaving the forest. As they ventured back out into the snow-covered fields, the temperature in the jammer slowly began to drop.

Pfc Cummings entertained the children with a well-redacted version of what had happened since they'd left the children in their shelter. He made sure to play up the adventure of Pfc Rodriguez. For his part, Rodriguez spent a few effort-filled moments trying to defend himself. The children were laughing too much for him to really make any headway.

"How's our direction, Sgt Fermo?" asked Cpl Larson

"Doing fine," said Imara. "You should be able to comm Maj Stewart or Cpl Hale. They can guide you in after that."

"You'll make it just fine, Sarge."

"Yes, I will." Imara wasn't sure who had said it, and she wasn't sure if it was a statement or question. But she had no plans of giving up, she just needed a medic and some rest.

"What's it like where you came from?" asked Cassandra.

"Where I came from? Do you mean the orphanage I grew up in? Or do you mean before we came to Abira?"

Cassandra wanted to know about Imara's experiences as an orphan, and her life in the orphanage on the world she'd come from. As Imara explained things to Cassandra, she began to understand what the girl was really doing. If Imara closed her eyes and went to sleep, she wouldn't be surprised if she never woke. Apparently, Cassandra had the same feeling. That may have partly been from having seen it happen before with her own family. That experience would have been enough that she would want to avoid repeating it. She may have also learned that keeping someone awake would keep them alive.

So, for Cassandra, Imara continued to answer the girl's questions even though it was becoming difficult to talk. About the time Imara had decided it didn't matter what question was going to be asked, she was going to sleep, the jammer came to a stop. The back door was cut free of the ropes and pulled from the door frame. Almost immediately after, people began piling out of the jammer box to be replaced by several medics that seemed to fill the space more than a half-dozen orphans had.

"Excuse us, young lady," said one of the medics.

Imara looked over at Cassandra. The girl's face lined with a worry that Imara thought might never disappear. Imara reached out and touched the girl's hand with her own. "It's okay," she said. "These guys are good at what they do."

"You got that right, Sergeant."

Imara patted Cassandra's hand. "So, I can rest now."

"Can she?" asked Cassandra. Imara could hear the tears in the girl's voice.

"She can," said one of the medics. "We'll keep her safe from here on."

Imara nodded agreement and closed her eyes.

22

One day later, Imara learned that when the landing beacon had been detected, the response from above had been precisely as she'd surmised earlier. The first dropships were on autopilot, dropping when the command was given. Shortly after that, there'd been a veritable onslaught of loaded dropships. They'd come from every ship in orbit. When they did come, they brought not only a regiment of troops but additional supplies. Those supplies included a really nice medical unit.

The medical unit was filled with all of the equipment that the medics and doctors needed to fix even the worst battlefield injuries, like Imara's. The technology and the medicines worked quickly, but even Imara had to stay stationary in a hospital recovery bed for several days.

Outside the medical facility, the snow continued to fall, and more supplies continued to be dropped in. There was no further attempt by the Rhone forces, who'd retreated into the falling snow. The snow made it nearly impossible to track the Rhone or where they went. But the Hospitallers knew one thing. The Rhone were definitely gone from the valley.

And thanks to modern medicine, four days later, Imara was on her feet, even if it was only light-duty allowed. Entering the inflated and heated barrack unit, she was met by her squad, who stood nervously behind Maj Stewart. The major had also come to greet her. The only problem with the major's presence was that Imara could not raise her arm to salute her commanding officer.

"I think that we can forgo the salute for now," said Major Stewart. "I came to see you because you still owe me four crawlers."

"I apologize for leaving them behind, Major," said Imara. "I'm pretty certain they're still there if you want me to go get them."

"That's part of the reason why I'm here. We're going to pay a visit to Grabouw and bring some supplies to replace those stolen by the Rhone soldiers. While we're there, I want to talk to the town council. And then we'll get my crawlers back. I wanted to see if you would like to come along?"

Imara now understood why the squad was nervous. They weren't afraid of anything bad, they were excited about another adventure. Sometimes it felt to her like they'd never grow up. None of them.

"I think a little drive through the country is just the kind of thing I need for my recovery, Major."

Major Stewart clapped his hands together, the sound muffled by thick gloves. He vigorously rubbed them together as he spoke. "Marvelous. We actually happen to have a couple rapid response vehicles standing by. Your squad is ready to go if you are?"

"If I don't have to pack anything," said Imara. "Then I guess I'm good to go."

Her squad cheered as they gathered around her as an escort to the nearest RapRes vehicle.

Rapid response vehicles weren't known for being comfortable transportation. Fortunately, Imara was still on pain blockers. It was also helpful that the RapRes wasn't charging into battle. Plus, it was moving over the snow-covered road versus the bumps created by the rock fences and hedgerows.

As the vehicles made their way toward the town of Grabouw, her squad caught her up on a few things she had missed. Most of it had to do with meals and Pfc Cummings's comedic antics. But they also told her about the orphans. A Shepherd had come down with one of the dropships to take care of them. It turned out there were several orphanages on planet though they weren't Hospitaller operated.

The orphans had been excited, looking forward to going to a Hospitaller orphanage. Instead, they were being shuttled to an Abira government-run orphanage, per the government's requests. Imara had a feeling that the little ones would be only mildly disappointed. Cassandra, on the other hand, who had proved herself by leading when it was just the children in a freezing house, would feel the lost opportunity the most.

If she had the chance, Imara would reach out to Cassandra. Maybe there'd be something she could do for her. She wasn't sure what, but she was a Hospitaller, she'd come up with something. Until then, she had her job to do, and they were finally entering Grabouw.

It had taken almost as long for the RapRes to reach Grabouw as it had the crawlers just a few days before. They'd been updated as they went along, informed by the sergeant operating the RapRes, as to their progress. So when they finally arrived in the center of the town, that, too, was announced by the driver.

As the rear gate of the RapRes was lowered, a burst of cold air and a swirl of falling snow found its way inside.

"I'd say that's really cold," said Pfc Cummings, who was closest to the lowering ramp. "But I have a new uniform on, and all of the heating elements work."

Imara had to agree with Pfc Cummings. It was much more pleasant to be out in the extended Abira winter when all of the heating elements in the uniform were working properly. She'd suffered from frostbite in several places because of the damaged heating elements in her old uniform. That had required several outpatient procedures to remediate. Fortunately, she was already in the hospital and had nothing better to do.

As Imara's squad exited the RapRes, they joined Maj Stewart, who'd been joined by Lt White. Another squad from the platoon was also present. Imara gave a nod to Sgt Johnson, who returned it with a grin. Behind Johnson and his squad, Imara saw four crawlers emerging from the falling snow.

A few meters away underneath a makeshift shelter that was already being buried in snow, stood the Grabouw town leaders. Despite the falling snow, Imara recognized the ones she'd previously met. The only person not present was Dmytro, and that did not surprise Imara.

Based on the looks of the Councilpersons present, the meeting was going to be as chilly as the snow-filled air around them.

Major Stewart marched through the falling snow to the waiting

Councilpersons and offered a hand. "Greetings. I'm Maj Stewart. I've brought you some more supplies as I've heard you lost the last load."

Imara couldn't miss the look on the Council people's faces as they chewed on their anger.

"What I really want is to tell you to take your supplies and go," said councilperson Ervik Baker. "But I have people here who need food to survive the rest of this blasted winter."

Major Stewart tilted his head and asked, "Why would you want to reject supplies if they are being offered freely?"

Councilperson Erig Hill leaned forward and said, "Because by accepting your supplies, we look like we're on your side. And your side is the Serdoban side, and that is not the side of our people, the Rhone."

"Now we look like traitors," said councilperson Baker.

"So the rest of the Rhone population would rather you and your town starve to prove your loyalty?" Asked major Stewart.

"They might just," said one of the councilpersons Imara hadn't met before.

Councilperson Baker held up a hand. The other councilperson bit off whatever else they were going to add. Baker said, "But we're not willing to die for their pride. We'll accept your aid and take our chances. But we will not be happy about the situation."

Major Stewart looked back at Imara and the other Hospitallers before turning his attention back to the councilpersons present. "We'll unload as quickly as possible and gather up all our missing crawlers. Then, we'll be out of here to save you further embarrassment."

"That suits us just fine." The four councilpersons turned and walked away, into the still-falling snow, and out of sight.

Major Stewart returned to the waiting Hospitallers, everybody already wearing a blanket of snow across their shoulders and helmet tops. "That went pretty well," said Major Stewart. "Any chance you know where to put these supplies?"

The End

Hello.

I hope that you've enjoyed reading Midwinter at Bhisho. This is the first book in the five book series, Seasons of War on Abira. Book two, Wintertide at Knynsa is out now (or will soon be). As for the rest? They are on their way, too.

If you want to be informed when the books are available, get a free story in the process, consider signing up for the Newsletter. You can go to www..earltroske.com where you'll find the link to join. You'll get a free story, too.

If it turns out that you enjoyed Midwinter at Bhisho, please consider leaving a review at your preferred vendor so that others can learn more about the book.

In the meantime, I'll be here in the San Francisco Bay area with my wife and daughter, and our standard poodle, writing every chance I get.

Until the next book.

Earl

www.ingramcontent.com/pod-product-compliance
Lightning Source LLC
Chambersburg PA
CBHW032211170626
46808CB00006B/2417